# WHERE YOU END

ANNA PELLICIOLI

# WHERE YOU END

Woodbury, Minnesota

First Edition
First Printing, 2015

Book design by Bob Gaul
Cover design by Ellen Lawson
Cover images: iStockphoto.com/12961162/©Borut Trdina

Flux, an imprint of Llewellyn Worldwide Ltd.

**Library of Congress Cataloging-in-Publication Data**
Pellicioli, Anna.
  Where you end/Anna Pellicioli.—First edition.
      pages cm
   Summary: Overwrought when she sees her ex-boyfriend with another girl during a class field trip, seventeen-year-old Miriam Feldman races into the Hirshhorn Sculpture Garden and pushes over a priceless Picasso sculpture, then finds herself blackmailed by the mystery girl who saw what she did.
   ISBN 978-0-7387-4403-2
[1. Extortion—Fiction. 2. Secrets—Fiction. 3. Vandalism—Fiction. 4. Dating (Social customs)—Fiction. 5. Family life—Washington (D.C.)—Fiction. 6. Jews—United States—Fiction. 7. Washington (D.C.)—Fiction.] I. Title.
   PZ7.1.P445Whe 2015
   [Fic]—dc23
                                                      2015002567

Flux
Llewellyn Worldwide Ltd.
2143 Wooddale Drive
Woodbury, MN 55125-2989
www.fluxnow.com

Printed in the United States of America

To Benjamin

# ONE

We forgot to cut our hair. We forgot to do our homework. We forgot to call our friends back. We spent whole afternoons diving into the skin of outstretched necks, sucked-in bellies, warm chests. When apart, we plotted where our fingers could climb our spines undisturbed, where we could crush each other next. We took turns leading each other into empty piano practice rooms and library stacks, and our bodies seemed to bond and bend to fit anywhere that would take us, like two inseparable rats.

We were two people sick in love, closing our paint-peeling shutters to the traffic outside as if the room would never need air, as long as we could breathe into it. So we did. Until someone opened the door and all that oxygen yanked him out into the world and slammed me back into the fire, where the burning is slow and steady.

———

I am Miriam, singing a song for the sorry women. He is Elliot, sharing museum fries with his new girl. We are over. It exhausts me.

———

Ms. D, the mastermind behind our junior year visit to the Smithsonian, announces we have an hour and a half for lunch and general meandering before the yellow bus zips us back to school. Everybody scatters to their corners of the National Mall. I have no business thumbing my dangly earrings by the triple-layer fountain or looking busy in front of the vending machine. I'm not looking forward to picking at cafeteria sushi on the steps behind the castle, trading bets on who will drink or fuck the most over the upcoming weekend, checking my back for boys who call each other gay for fun. Those are not my girls and boys.

I liked the bass player who could do math, the guy who craves falafel and scribbles fantasy playlists in a Moleskine he keeps in his back pocket. E is for Elliot, extra excruciating. An artist, a music man, someone with depth. I wanted more, you know, like the Little Mermaid.

And I got it, the whole deal—the love, the sex, the decay. All of it. I know everybody wants that. Well, I got it, and I lost it. Now at least I can write you a sad song with some depth.

"Hey Meem, come over here."

It's Adam, my best friend pre-Elliot, fellow photography enthusiast, the only guy who can wear a T-shirt with a Renoir painting and not get any crap for it. "Meem" is the name he gave me after our first summer developing photos in my basement darkroom, back when we thought pictures of busted bicycles were cool. It's stuck for over four years now. I drag my feet close enough to smell burnt coffee on him. It's the first time I feel okay all morning. I want to plant my nose in his curly hair.

"There's a Winogrand exhibit at the Gallery. Let's get a hot dog or something and go," he says.

Winogrand is one of the greatest storytellers of all time. Almost every Winogrand picture is interesting, whether it's the light, the subject, the angle, or the timing that holds your gaze.

"I don't know, Adam. Maybe. I'll think about it."

Adam's brick house is five blocks after my yellow one, but we never spoke until Hebrew school, in sixth grade. We were the only two kids who hadn't been there since kindergarten. His mom is Jewish and his Dad is Quaker. My parents are both Jewish, but they call themselves humanist Jews. Basically, it means they think Judaism is less about God and more about people and their story.

My parents are big on stories and roots and knowing where you come from. They think religion is about dignity, family, and looking for some kind of truth. They're big on truth. That's why we do Shabbat even though we don't follow most other rules, why they sent me to read the Torah when I turned twelve. So that I could remember I have a soul as well as a history. It's fine with me. Winogrand was Jewish too.

"Maybe?" Adam says, interrupting my scrambled thoughts. "You'll think about it? What's wrong with you, Meem? What else are you gonna do? You know Winogrand's your favorite."

"Lange is my favorite, Adam," I remind him.

His huge brown eyes roll. The lazy left one lags a little. "Lange is fucking depressing."

Adam could say the Hebrew curse words better than any other pimply-ass kid in that room, and he read the Torah with enough confidence to earn everybody's respect, even the Rabbi's, who generally disapproved of us late-comers. He knew what the words meant too. His mother promised him a camera for his bar mitzvah, and he earned that thing fair and square. That's the year I got my darkroom. After we became friends, we spent every other day messing with baths and light in my basement, talking about our favorite photographers. We agreed on Winogrand.

"It's the 1964 pictures, Meem. You sure?" he says now, and his voice betrays that impatient pity, the kind that's been haunting me since I broke up with Elliot.

The 1964 pictures were taken the year Winogrand got a grant and used it to travel across the country. They're a portrait of a country I don't really know, but many of them are impossible to forget. They look so real, like a real piece of the culture, like they could only be taken in that moment, in that place. It's what every photographer wishes they could do.

"I don't know, Adam. Maybe. I may just hang around here … "

"Come on … "

I don't know what to say. Sometimes it feels like I'm on a deadline and if I don't cheer up soon, they might all leave me. It blows to be around a sad person, and it blows most if they used to be your best friend, or your adventurous, smart daughter.

I consider how much I love the 1964 Winogrand photos, especially the picnic in the desert. There's a beautiful white car, the kind with fins and a wide rear end, and it's parked in the middle of the White Sands Desert. The car is next to a picnic shelter that looks like it's from the future. There's a family too, a couple of kids and a woman, maybe in a red shirt, and they are all walking toward a grill, in the middle of a desert. The only scenery is the sand and the sky—a family stopping for lunch in the middle of sand and sky. It's unreal, but it happened. I imagine Winogrand, the photographer, stopping his own car to capture the scene, thinking: only here, only now.

As I remember all that bright light, I start to feel nauseous, like the more I try to focus, the more I lose my balance. This is not the first time. I've been getting sick quite a bit lately, so I know what usually happens next. I shake my head quickly, nod goodbye, and hurry to find the nearest museum bathroom, where I elbow my way through the people who check in and out of my city every day.

When I get to the toilet, nothing comes out, so I stare at the cloudy water and wave my hand in front of the little laser just to see it flush clean. I know what nausea can mean for a girl who used to sleep with a boy. Never mind. I'm alone again. I can stand up. Everything smells like bleach.

By the time I get back outside, I'm hungry. I can see Adam walking toward the exhibit. He's about a block away. His arms are all long and loose at his sides, the way boys seem to have more gravity but less weight, their long limbs dragging and swinging and falling to the earth. Not like girls, who keep everything close to their body. I follow his backpack like it's a red shiny bug getting smaller and smaller.

I know what's in there. Extra batteries, a notebook, music, an old city map, maybe a snack, definitely a drink, his tiny leather wallet, coins all over his front pocket. I haven't looked in there for a long time. Still, I know. We were that close. Adam turns around, and I wince. I don't want him to catch me looking, but there are no trees to hide behind. Everything is so open here. He doesn't seem to see me. I blend too well with the gravel and the buildings.

A girl I know from English class (short hair, enviable breasts, mildly interesting insights) is walking toward him. Adam motions for her to catch up. His camera strap is wrapped around his wrist. That's how he always holds it— ready to shoot. It seems offensive today, out in the daylight like that, and Adam suddenly annoys me.

The girl (what the hell is her name?) runs ahead and stops to face him, begging for a picture. She sticks her ass out a little, one hand on her hip. He shakes his head, then gives in with a smile. He got her. Never mind Winogrand

and his picnic. Adam's not going to miss me. The ladies love a mystery art man. I should know.

I turn away to find a good spot to attempt lunch. So far, the sea sickness has killed my appetite, but I can't bring myself to throw the food away. My mother has been packing my lunch for the past two months. She taught me how to make my own sandwiches when I was four, and now she sends me off with a brown bag every day. She's worried I'm losing weight, and she has a point.

I should take at least one bite. I opt for the carousel and find the bench with the least pigeon shit, where I sit and reach into my bag for last night's dinner. I dig for her sandwich under the flashlight, my camera, my extra sweater, and the half-empty Nalgene bottle. I had no time to unpack this morning.

The sun bounces off the tinfoil, forcing my swollen eyes shut.

It's roast beef, mustard, soggy green beans—leftovers from last night's dinner. The bread is a little stale, but not as bad as I imagined. I toss the crumbs to the birds hiding under the curled steel and watch an old man buy a carousel ride from a bored beauty, who slips him tickets under the grate. A little guy is waiting anxiously at the entrance, and they look like the only riders around, so I doubt they'll run the carousel just for them.

The old man hands the tickets over to an attendant and tips his veteran baseball cap in a gesture that belongs to a town where you can still get your cream soda at the counter. I imagine him coming home to a parade like the one in that

Times Square picture, kissing his girlfriend after the war, balloons flying everywhere, brass blowing the whole block up, lots of Jimmies looking for their Betsies. All while my mom's Opa sighs six million times in a Brooklyn tenement.

They're in. Looking for the perfect horse, the little dude slips under bellies and past peeling hooves to mount his very own pink stallion. Grandpa suggests the brown one instead, but the boy is fifty years ahead, and when he hops on his pink steed, he grabs those reins like he plans to bop all the way up to Congress. *Wheeeeee.* The old man keeps his trembling fingers on the boy's back the whole time. With each turn, I look for them, and each time, there they are.

No matter how many times I see the boy's sloppy grin, when he disappears into the music, I can hardly wait to see him again. For a second, I wish my life could be more like this, and I promise God that I would let everything go if only I could be sure it would come back after one round of waltz. Once, the boy looks at me and waves, but he's gone by the time I wave back. I try again on the next round, but he's distracted now. I'm so vain that when the carousel stops and the boy hollers, I actually think it may be for me.

As grandpa ushers the kid away, I notice something on the ground and walk over to check it out. A silver money clip: *With Love, from Sarah, Christmas 1989.*

"Excuse me, sir, did you lose this?"

He's frazzled for a minute, but then he looks at me with that old-man curtain over his eyes.

"My mother's name is Sarah," I say, immediately ashamed of having read the engraving.

But the old man calls me "peach." I mean, he refers to me as a peach. He says, "Thank you. You're a peach." And I swear I feel like a peach when I turn back around, all fuzzy and sweet and in season, and what can a peach do but reach for her beat-up Nikon, still hot from last night. The lens cap fell off somewhere. It must have been later than usual. I adjust the aperture, but it takes a minute to remember the math. I haven't taken a picture in daylight since the Fourth of July, but this feels like something worth looking at. The pink horse will be flattered.

I hang the strap around my neck, to be safe.

A line has formed outside the gate, and the attendant is now a bouncer. The carousel plays a waltz and the parents hum along and check their text messages while the little ones get dizzy. I scan for the horse and find Elliot instead, my Elliot, on a black mare with no tail. He's laughing. His long, skinny legs dangle below the plastic saddle and one hand is wrapped around the gold pole. On the next round, I spot Maggie Sawyer, more specifically Maggie's teeth, then Maggie's curls, then Maggie's hands reaching over to grab Elliot's. While spinning, they tangle their fingers and they smile, and my mouth is suddenly full of bile.

I start running so hard and clumsy I don't notice the camera pounding my chest until my feet have hit the ramp that leads down to the Hirshhorn sculpture garden and someone yells *slow down*. Then I remember I have hands, legs, feet, and, somewhere in there, even a pulse.

I shove my camera back into my bag where it belongs and circle the garden, trying to calm down. Most people must have left for lunch because I can't hear anything except for the dull noise of my head tightening, the sound of a knot. I'm still reeling from the waltz of horrors when I round the corner to find Picasso, mocking me with a woman made of bronze. I think of how many times I've held Elliot's hand, how exactly it feels in mine, where his hair starts, how warm it always was. I put my palms out to touch the sculpture, but the bronze is freezing.

I pull my hand back and look at the woman. She is standing at attention; her arms point straight down, but she has no hands—just fists, balled-up fists. Her legs and arms are bumpy, and so is her face. The metal wrinkles around her shoulders and her tiny features. Her neck is thick, but her face is small and flat; you can hardly see her eyes. The only smooth parts are her belly and her breasts. I think of my own body naked, of Elliot, of Elliot looking at my body, of how sure I felt after the first few times, how powerful, how skilled, how wanted.

I feel deep and insidious shame. I wonder if he's seen Maggie too, if she's let him touch her in the same places, if they ever did it without a condom. I reach up to push the sculpture a little, against her calves. She doesn't move. Unaffected. Permanent. She won't even look at me. I notice her feet, huge and unfinished, melting into the pedestal. A man's feet, a monster's feet. The garden is quiet. My friends are far away. I reach up, close my eyes, and push, with my whole self. She barely resists. The whole thing gives, and thumps on the grass below. I hear something snap. My teeth finally let go of my lip, and I realize I have been crying. I run as fast as I can up the steps, to the street.

When I reach the top, I look back for a second. I can't tell if anything is broken, but she's on the ground, lying on her back, looking up at the clear sky in an impossible position. I knocked her down. A few tourists are gasping at the body, and a security guard is trying to lift her from the head. Her smile has not faded in the least. She seems amused, actually, almost like she's been waiting to get a different angle.

Another guard runs up and clears people away from the scene, as if someone's just had a horrible accident—someone with bones and lungs and blood. The guards lay the sculpture back down together. A few people shake their heads and walk on. The men talk into their gadgets, probably calling for help. They gesture and shrug and run their hands through their hair. They've decided it's best not to touch her.

A girl in a T-shirt walks on the grass and stands next to the body. My heart smacks my chest. The girl leans over the belly. A guard tells her to step away and she backs off; then she looks up toward me and back at the sculpture. I turn around and walk slowly away, counting to ten, trying not to look suspicious. There's no way she knows. I run, without looking back, even once. I would've pushed harder, I think, had I known metal would give like that.

# TWO

I find my breath in front of the command module that carried Aldrin and his men to the moon and back. It looks so much smaller than it did when I was the kid reading the placard. It's the same blue carpet at the Air and Space, the same smell of armpits and dust from second grade. The only difference is that everything's shrunk a little, especially the Columbia. This is the safest place I could think of. It's hard to tell if anybody is after me. I wouldn't know what to look for. I consider climbing into the module and making like I'm Michael Collins, fogging up the space helmet and reporting back to my own Houston.

But I remember Michael Collins was a putz, taking pictures of the lunar surface while his buddies bounced around making small steps and giant leaps. The man drove the thing through the Earth's atmosphere, scorched a layer in five-thousand-degree heat, and when he came home to his wife and she asked him *was it cold on the moon, what did the moon feel like, how did you like the moon,* all he got to say is *it was spectacular, honey, from the window of my command module.* I don't want to be Michael Collins.

I may be a vandal, and they'll arrest me or make me do community service, and I will never get into college, but if I drive myself to the moon, I will not hide in the fucking spaceship.

So far, I have no missed calls, no handcuffs, no fat police officer telling me to sit down in a room without windows. Just the image of a woman with a small head and very little face. When I close my eyes, I see bronze. When I open them, my pale, shaky hands. I have to think. *Focus that lens,* Adam would say. I buy a ticket for the next planetarium show and settle into a center seat, where my memory explodes like a ball of hot gas.

Elliot played the upright bass in the jazz band, and I had seen him lugging that monster into the music room on Wednesdays, practice day. I learned to get to school a little late those mornings, to time it so I could watch him drag the instrument in and maybe work my way up from a nod to a smile, even a word. I didn't love him yet, obviously, but his boyish face, the sleepy green eyes, the whole Wednesday ritual became a resource for me, something to space out about on the bus ride home, a reason to hold my hair up and study my crooked mouth in the bathroom after brushing my teeth. I am a photographer. I see people; and then I want to keep them. All I knew was his name. It took us many Wednesdays to make any real contact.

The day we finally spoke it was snowing, but our school stayed open, and we were two of a handful of students who showed up. Half the teachers stayed home. Elliot and I didn't have any classes together, and I figured band practice would be cancelled, but I didn't protest when my father asked me to help shovel the car out.

We did the whole thing with a cookie sheet and a spatula, so by the time we got to school I was sure I'd missed Elliot. Shaking the snow off my boots, feeling the rising disappointment, I reminded myself of how smart I actually was. I read biographies. I played a decent game of Scrabble. I could hold my own in a music-snob rant. I had friends and a more-than-decent shot at art school. The boy snuck up.

"It's just the two of us, I think."

The scratchy voice was right behind me, and I stole a second before turning around, smiling right through my frosted cheeks. I had expected the register to be lower (yes, more like a bass) and I was glad I still had enough wits to find that thought funny.

"I mean here, at school," he clarified, stomping his own snowy heels on the mat. No bass, just a big wool scarf he uncoiled off his neck in a way that made me need to look away.

"I know," I said. "My mom made me come."

*My mom made me come.* My mom made me come. My mom can't even make me finish what's on my plate these days.

He said he thought the snow was pretty, and I agreed with a smile.

"After you, Miriam."

My name sounded so pure and full, like I was the first Miriam, *his* Miriam. It's what I miss the most, the sound of my name in his mouth. I spent the rest of that day letting Elliot's voice bounce like a dollar-store ball inside my empty head. *Miriam* in the chemistry lab, *Miriam* in American History, *Miriam* in French Literature, *Miriam* in Trigonometry, *Miriam* in the darkroom.

When school let out, the snow had stopped and settled everywhere, and I took a moment to pull up my hood and tease out my bangs before starting out toward the bus stop. Our rides were stuck at home under a new coat of frost. As I tucked my jeans into my boots, I noticed letters in the snow:

WAIT FOR ME

And in parentheses that should have alarmed me:

(PLEASE)

It could have been for anybody, but this is my story, and that was my moment, and I wanted someone to want me to wait. So I waited.

When Elliot came out, he puffed his breath in the cold and asked how I was getting home. I told him the buses were probably stuck, and, with his hands in his prep school coat pockets, he motioned to the street with his shoulder. We stepped right over the snow message and just walked, my gray sweater to his blue coat, all the way there. We talked about what we saw: little kids licking their gloves, the empty streets at rush hour, angels on the dirty sidewalks, the pizza delivery guy brushing snow off his bike with his bare hands.

We must have looked happy. I bet we looked handsome.

I blush like a Polish girl when it's cold out and my hair straightens out and sticks to my face. Elliot's lips turn sort of blue. He hunched his shoulders to keep warm, like my father's Bob Dylan on the cover of *Freewheelin'*, and sometimes we bumped into each other, gently, to slow it all down. I learned he liked music. He learned I liked pictures. When we got to my place, two candles were lit in the menorah behind my window and neither one of us had mentioned the writing in the snow.

Dad was home early and my parents were shuffling between the kitchen and the living room, busy in the evening buzz. Elliot and I stood outside on the porch, like in the movies.

"That's nice, the candles."

"Thanks, it's for Hanukkah."

"You light a candle every night?"

"Every night for eight days."

"Why eight days?"

"That's how long it took for the light to come back"

That was our first kiss. I can still feel the porch light flooding us, but our voices now blend in my head. I try hard to focus on the memory of that day. I sit up a little in my planetarium chair, tune out the narrating voice, and think hard, trying to taste the salt in that kiss we had in honor of the Maccabean revolt. Had I looked up that night, I would have seen the stars fretting, shrieking *this is no miracle, no wonder, no salvation.*

Instead, I closed my eyes and took the kiss with everything that came after. No regrets. According to this program and its soothing narrator, by the time I could've heard the stars' advice, the universe would have already expanded. The concept comforts me. It's not my fault things keep moving.

As the lights turn back on and my eyes adjust to the missing stars, I let people walk past me to the exit. Fear hits me in neck-breaking waves. I have only a few seconds to think before the next swell of panic rolls over me. What time is it? What if somebody knows? How long have they been waiting? Should I confess? What are they going to do to me? Did I mention I had a decent shot at art school?

There is a line of visitors waiting to see the next show, and, either way, it's time for me to go home. A lady in uniform walks in to take out the trash. I have to move, but I'm frozen in that chair. The lady doesn't see me. I think she's listening to music. Maybe I can just stay and listen to the voice again. Maybe if I watch the stars enough times, I won't feel so scared. This is, after all, what they mean when they say "the great scheme of things."

A hand rests on my shoulder, and I let out a small shriek.

"Sorry," the girl behind me says.

"No, no. I'm sorry," I say, laughing a little, as I take in the very first sketch of this stranger. She's probably my age, maybe a little bit older. Her hair is black and thick. She drops her smile.

"So … we don't have a lot of time," she says, as her head nods toward the door.

Her voice is husky but young, like she's getting over a sore throat. There's a strange rhythm to it, like English may not quite be her first language. I stay silent and in my chair. Her voice lowers to a whisper.

"I saw what you did," she says.

Now I want to run. More than I did when I pushed the sculpture, when my body did the escaping for me. This feels nothing like a dream. Every surface is flooding; there's an ocean in my fingers, my belly, my hair. Since getting up doesn't seem like a real option, I turn around to face the front and think, but she jumps over the chairs to sit right next to me.

"Do you know how much that thing is worth?" she says. I keep quiet. I get the feeling these aren't questions I'm actually expected to answer.

"It's a Picasso," she says, shaking her head and looking for my face. "It must be millions."

She takes a breath and looks ahead, settling back into her chair. We're just sitting there, the two of us. Whoever she is, whoever I am. Two minutes ago, total strangers, and now she knows my biggest secret and, worst of all, I know she knows it. My phone vibrates. It's so quiet in the dome that we can both hear it. I leave it in my bag and let it ring a few times. I don't want this girl to touch anything else in my life.

"Go ahead," she says. "You can get it. I'll wait. Just try to make it quick, 'cause the next group is coming in soon."

I get the feeling I'm following orders, but I reach for the

phone anyway. It's my mom, telling me I'm half an hour late for the bus and everyone is freaking out. Once she calms down, I reassure her I'll be at the bus soon. I'm sure someone called her, probably Adam or Ms. D or the school counselor. I have two other missed calls, but I'm not going to check who it is right now. I silence the thing and bury it back in my bag.

"I gotta go," I say, avoiding the girl's face.

"We have to talk before you go," she says.

"I'm late," I say.

"Right. You have to go back to Sterling."

Now I look at her. She knows the name of my school; she saw me push the sculpture; she obviously followed me in here.

"Look," she says, "I saw you push the Picasso, but I don't think anybody else saw."

I can't tell if this is supposed to make me feel better.

"What do you want?" I say, trying to keep my tone as even as possible.

"I don't know yet," she says, "but I'll figure it out."

She's rubbing her necklace; a gold fish. A fish made of gold.

"I don't know what you saw," I say, "but I really have to go now."

"You know what I saw. I saw you. I saw you run down the ramp. I saw you walk around the garden. I saw you put your hands on that sculpture, on the Picasso, and then I saw you push. I saw the thing fall down and you running again. I saw you. And I'm not going to forget you, and you're not going to forget me."

She lets the fish drop against her brown skin. I want to cry. I can feel the tears coming up. I cannot cry in front of this girl.

"Look, I'm just saying that I think we can help each other," she says, a little softer but still determined.

"I don't even know who you are," I say.

She says her name is Paloma and holds out her hand. I'm calling bullshit. That's Picasso's daughter, and I don't believe in cosmic coincidence, so she's definitely messing with me. Her hand is still hanging.

"Maggie." I sit up and shake her hand.

"Maggie," she says, looking up at the blank dome again, "do you believe in God?"

Dead fucking serious.

"Probably," I say. "Yes. I guess I do."

"Me too," she says. "That must be a good sign, right?"

Another rhetorical question. I am pretty sure we're not the only two people who believe in God.

"You know where the National Cathedral is?" she asks.

"Yeah."

"Great. Let's meet there on Sunday, at two. I'll know what I want then."

I sit there, helpless, thinking about the choices I don't have. That's when she takes my hand, rolls up my sleeve, and writes her phone number on my arm.

"We should go," Paloma says, nodding over to the open doors and the people filing in. I'm first, so I lead the way out, not looking back, but very much aware of this girl behind me, presumably my only witness, who thinks we are bound by a moment of complete rage. I think I feel her hand on my back, guiding me past the entering crowd, but I must be imagining it because, when I get out and finally look back, she is nowhere in sight.

I pick up the pace toward the bus, trying not to run, pretending everything is under control. I can't help but go over everything in my head, from the sculpture to the planetarium. She said the sculpture is probably worth millions. Of course, I knew that. I'm the daughter of an art gallery owner, a curator. I spent my first year of life drooling in museums. My mother is a photographer; her mother was a painter, and, before Elliot and Picasso, I was counting on an art scholarship. I was raised to think art is the stuff humans are made of. This is not just about the millions. It's about breaking somebody's work. It's about punching Picasso, arguably the greatest artist in modern history, in the fucking nose.

"Where the hell were you?" Adam walks toward me.

The girl from before is not with him. He looks enormous, his chest right in the trajectory of my face. Maybe if I get a head start I could break into it, lodge myself between his lungs and his heart and never ever deal with what is outside. Maybe we could hide like we did when we were younger. I bet it's warm in there. I bet Paloma would not find me.

"I got sick," I say. "I mean, I don't feel good."

"Yeah, you look like shit. I tried to call you. What's with your phone?"

Oh Adam. Do you know that only one percent of stars are massive enough to explode into a Supernova? That the life of a star depends on its mass, what it's filled with, that most stars end up white dwarfs? Do you know that if it wasn't for time we would all still be stars? I was trying to stop time; that's what I was doing. Someone caught me trying to stop time.

"Battery's dead," I say.

"Everybody's pretty pissed. Your mom's worried. We had to call her after forty-five minutes of waiting here."

Forty-five minutes is a while. I could have been gone in forty-five minutes.

"Okay," I say, "I'm sorry. How was the Winogrand?"

Adam looks confused. "How was Winogrand ... Meem, what's wrong with you? You're late. You didn't call anybody. There's a bus full of people waiting. Winogrand was crowded and awesome. Where were you?"

"Can you tone down the yelling? I told you—I don't feel good, Adam. I had to sit down."

"Sorry. I was just a little worried. We didn't know where you were. I looked everywhere."

You didn't look in outer space, my friend, not in space, where Picasso's daughter hunts you down and asks you if you believe in God. She could have been a ghost, or some kind of divining angel. She could be whatever appears after you fuck up—to help you find your way again.

"Anyway, watch out," Adam warns me. "Ms. D is in a really shitty mood. Someone pushed a sculpture in the garden and the guards cornered her about it. They told her they wanted to call the school. They were trying to blame it on one of us because we were the only group of kids around. How fucked up is that? Like, hey, someone knocked a Picasso, it must be some dumbass kid from Sterling with nothing better to do ... "

"Pretty fucked up ... " I mutter.

"It was a Picasso, for godssake. That's got to be hundreds of thousands of dollars."

I start to correct him, then hold my tongue. Adam is walking really fast. He's not listening anyway.

He's telling his story.

"Ms. D lost it. Went on and on about how she knows her students and how dare they suggest and why not ask the bored tourists ... You should have seen it. She was sharp. I think the leather jacket's getting to her."

"How did they know someone pushed it?"

"What?" he says, confused.

"How do they know it didn't just fall?" I ask.

Adam tucks his chin in.

"Meem, you of all people know a sculpture doesn't just fall. It's *attached*. With a metal rod. On a pedestal. The wind didn't knock her down. She probably hit the wall on the way down. Can you imagine? It was on the ground. I saw it."

"You saw it?" I ask. Then I stop and remember. The girl in the T-shirt. The look. Nobody else was wearing a T-shirt. That was Paloma.

"Was it broken?" I ask.

"I'm not sure. It was kind of nice actually, in a morbid way. You would've wanted a picture."

Adam looks at me, smiles, and turns my shoulders toward the bus. "Let us go, my friend," he says, and we walk toward Ms. D and the rest of the impatient circus.

As she walks toward me, Ms. D's face is too stiff to read. Could Ms. D know what happened? Maybe that's why she was so defensive.

"Miriam, get on the bus and call your mother please," she says.

I hold the phone in my hand and consider the chances of Ms. D bluffing. No chaperone likes to take responsibility for vandalism. This would be a disaster for the school. *Heartbroken artsy girl attacks bronze woman. Privileged student beats defenseless sculpture. Teenage angst knocks down timeless art.* Maybe Ms. D knows, and she's just buying time.

"I'm sorry, Ms. D. I got sick."

"We'll deal with it later, when we get to school. Call your mom."

"We already spoke," I say.

Ms. D rolls her eyes and tells me to just get on the bus. No "please" this time.

Elliot must be inside. I know he is. That's how this whole thing started, even if the carousel seems so long ago, a place I can't get to anymore, a door that's been shut by the timeline. The last time I felt this kind of urgency was with Elliot. But when I remember he's not mine to confess to, instead of feeling disappointed I feel a delicious calm come over me, as if all this fear has a purpose I haven't discovered yet. All that bigness narrows and, like a needle, I focus and point. I know something you don't know. I'm late because I pushed a priceless work of art. You don't know me.

I follow Adam up into the bus and slip through a few whispers, but most of the class is already lost in a sea of music, their headphones like garlands across their heavy heads. Elliot and Maggie have settled in the back, his scarf around her neck, her hair on his shoulder. They are not talking. They could be on a riverboat in Paris, on a jeep in the Serengeti.

Wherever they are, they're together, looking out. I twist my hair into a loose bun. It's always been tangled enough to stay tied. I see the phone number on my arm again, but instead of hiding it under the sweater, I let my arm drop to my side. Let them see it. I stare at Elliot and Maggie. I'm not scared. My secret soothes me. Maggie is distracted, but I catch Elliot's eyes. He closes them to shut me out. Adam tugs at my sweater.

"Meem, sit down."

Someone saw what I did, but they haven't told on me yet. Someone saw what I did, but they want to talk to me first. Someone saw what I did and they think it means something. We can help each other, the girl said. She'll know what she wants.

"Hey Adam," I say, "what do you know about Picasso?"

"He's dead. Will you sit?

I sit and smile.

First, there was dark matter. The beginning was pitch black.

# THREE

In our kitchen, my mother looks up deviled eggs in *The Art of Simple Food*.

"Stuffed eggs," she says with her finger on the recipe index. "Stuffed eggs."

She rubs the grease off the side of her nose, a sign of worry.

I know them well, the signs. Driving with both hands on the wheel, buying a new plant at the nursery, eating chips out of a pretty ceramic bowl, loading the dishwasher before we've finished dessert, dog-earing furniture catalogues, looking up a recipe she's made a hundred times. My mother is a coping machine. And despite her efforts to keep it together, my job is to try and pull her apart like a pack of frozen chicken breasts. I used to justify it as a way of reminding my mother she was human, but now it feels like I'm pounding her just because I can.

"Miriam. Come here."

She turns the faucet on with her wrists, to wash off any raw egg, and instructs me to sit down on one of the mismatched chairs around our kitchen table. I choose the yellow one with the teetering leg.

"Hi."

"Hi."

"So?"

"So."

"What happened?" she says.

The controlled tone would be scary if I didn't know this technique. It feels familiar and safe. I sink back to my role in our game.

"I was late."

She's using a needle to poke one hole on the bottom of each eggshell. She waits until she's finished to look up. Good. She's going to play.

"Why were you late?" she says.

"I kind of got lost."

"On the Mall?"

"Yes."

A variety of herbs are laid out on a clear cutting board: basil, parsley, chives. They come from little pots on the kitchen windowsill. It's usually my job to pick them. When I was a kid, if I gave her the wrong one, Mom would put it in my pocket so I could smell it all day until I knew the difference between cilantro and parsley, lavender and rosemary. I was also a sort of prodigy in the produce section. More than once, I remember sticking my face in a green plastic bag and, with great confidence, declaring the name of an obscure vegetable.

"Adam said you were sick," she says.

She rolls the basil up into little green cigarettes, preparing to slice them and let the magic out of the leaves. Once I got old enough to use a knife, that was my favorite part. I teeter back and forth on the yellow chair's lame leg. Adam must've called her after the bus.

"Adam doesn't know."

"Doesn't know what?"

"Doesn't know anything."

"Doesn't know anything?"

"Doesn't know why."

"Why what?"

"Why I was late."

"You said you got lost."

"Yes."

The timer rings eight minutes, and she dips a slotted spoon in the pot, fishes out an egg, and drops it carefully in a bowl of cold water. Six times.

"He was worried," she says.

"I know. He worries."

"So, were you sick or were you lost?"

Normally, before Elliot, this is when I would give up and remember my mother's heart is painfully accurate, most of the time. And I would join her at the sink, help peel the eggs and drop my guns. I would tell her what happened, how I'm feeling, who said what at school and why they shouldn't have, and how we read this great story and someone made a stupid comment, and I can't wait to get out of high school etcetera, etcetera, etcetera. And she would nod and laugh her deep strong laugh and remind me that everyone is different, Miriam, but we all deserve the same respect. But I would know, instinctively, what that actually means: that she thinks I'm smarter than everyone else, and so I should oblige.

Before Elliot, this is when I would spill.

Today I can't. Today I keep quiet about the carousel and Picasso and Paloma, because this feels like my problem, like it's more than what she could possibly understand. Something separates her life from mine. Maybe this is what happens after you fall in love.

When you start out, if you're lucky, your parents are the closest thing you have to yourself. They're your safe spot, your personal believers. Then, if you're lucky again, you meet a guy who makes you feel like you might be different than what you imagined, more … like everything in your body has a purpose and that purpose comes to life when he's around. Only when he's around.

All of a sudden, he's the only one in the entire world who knows you, so nothing is ever the same. You come home, and your parents kiss you in that spot on your head where they've always kissed you, but they don't know. They sit at the same table and make the same jokes, but they don't know what's in your head. They don't know your laugh and who it's for. Not anymore. It's not your hands they're holding, your face they're kissing, your voice they're listening to. They are loving a memory.

Only you know the present tense, the stuff that makes

your blood move and your lungs work. All of that belongs to the person you just said goodbye to, the guy who you can still smell on your shirt. And you don't recover from that. Even after the guy drops you. They still can't know you anymore.

Mom peels off the shells and dumps them into the disposal on her own, and I get chills from the sound of them crick-cracking into egg dust.

"I heard there's a Winogrand exhibit at the Gallery," she says, before I can make my escape.

"Really?"

"Really. Is that where you were, Miriam?"

"Yes," I say, grateful for an honorable way out. Of course that's where I was.

"You lost track of time at the Gallery?"

"Yes," I say, pretending to give in, sort of soft and dejected, the best kind of fake.

You got me, Mom. I was actually looking at photographs, just like you would've been, just like you do every day. I was studying the masters. I got lost in the art. It was *that* good.

"It was the 1964 photos, right?" she asks as she scoops out the yolks and leaves twelve little rowboats wiggling on the board.

I can tell she's struggling to rein in her excitement. Only a genius skips the field trip to gaze at modern art. And everybody wants a genius, no matter how deviant.

"Yes. It was amazing. They had all the best pictures, the white sands picnic and everything."

"No?"

"Yes," I sputter like a faucet that's been turned off for too long, my lies the brown muck. "The Daley Plaza, the lady with the pink headband ... "

"The woman in the garage."

"Exactly. The woman in the garage, with the baby. That one is gorgeous."

There's a word you don't hear every day at the Feldmans'. Certainly never to describe a photograph. Mom should smell this one, but she stays quiet.

"Where's the mayo?" I ask, all puffed up from my perfect fib.

"I'm doing olive oil tonight," she says. "I'm glad you liked it so much—the exhibit. You should've told me the truth though, Miriam ... "

I nearly choke on my own spit.

"It's important," she says. "There's nothing wrong with going to see art, but you should've been on time, and you should've told me the truth."

I breathe out.

"I know, I know. I'm sorry. He's my favorite, you know. I got caught up."

"Lange is your favorite," she says.

Then she flips her palm, drops all the green bits into the yolks and starts stirring, never lifting her head from the bowl, waiting for me to rescue myself. My silence always wins, though, because she's the mother, and I'm her baby, and she's the one who's left with the worry. All my mother can do is rip a page out of her cookbook and shove it under the wooden leg of my chair.

"There," she says.

And, for a minute, I feel sad the chair is the only thing we can get straight in this house. Sad for my mother, not for me.

# FOUR

Across the street, our neighbor walks past a couple of plastic tombstones, high-fives Frankenstein, and reaches up the tree to turn on his polyester ghost. Mr. Wallace stands under the white sheet for a minute or so, to make sure it's howling properly. I move closer to the window and figure about half the leaves are off our gingko. Last time I really looked at the tree, it was full of fruits that smell like sewage. Now they are thousands of miniature yellow fans covering our front yard. *Ooooooohhhhhhhhh. OOOOOhhhhhhhhhh,* the ghost cries. My elbow is on the windowsill, and I'm watching it turn green, blue, and then white once more. The dishes rattle in the sink downstairs. The sun is setting. This is the view from my window. This is what I know.

My first real photo teacher always told us to take pictures of what we know. Stay close to home, he said, where it hurts to look. I wasn't sure what that meant, but now

I'm getting closer to understanding. I watch Mr. Wallace walk back through the fake cobwebs toward his house.

I'm so tired I can barely hear the kitchen clatter downstairs, but when I lie down to sleep, everything suddenly conspires to keep me awake. I can't tune out the second hand tick-tocking on my watch. I take the watch off, and my ears start ringing a mean ring, like the batteries in my head have gone out. A dog barks. The computer hums. It doesn't matter that I took everything off my walls the minute I got home from Elliot's beach house—the photographs, the F-stop cheat sheet, the books off the shelves and the shelves off the wall. This empty room still haunts me.

I went to Ace Hardware by myself. I brought home painter's tape, a brush, and many quarts of dirty green paint. I did the whole room in one morning, while my parents were at the farmer's market buying heirloom tomatoes the size of your face. When they came back and saw the walls, my mom's eyes started twitching and my father dropped the rhubarb.

"It's the Atlantic Ocean," I told them.

Someone knocks to interrupt my memory. I shut my eyes, breathing deep to feign sleep. The door squeaks open and Dad whispers my name. I picture my lids smooth and angelic. I float my tongue in my mouth to fake peace. He tiptoes out and I listen for his feet down the stairs, toward the dining room.

I run to the bathroom and roll up my sleeve to erase Paloma's writing, but when I reach for the soap I can't bring myself to do it. It happened. She wasn't a ghost. I turn off the water and get my phone to dial the number. It goes straight to voicemail. Instead of Paloma's voice, a little boy comes on. He tells me I've reached the number on my arm and tells me to leave a message. A girl laughs in the background.

"Miriaaaaaam. Dinner."

Mom's call makes it past the floorboards, through the carpet, under my door. I hang up the phone right after the beep. It's Friday—the linen tablecloth, the heavy silverware, the challah, and the wine. We don't go to temple, but my parents take the weekly dinner pretty seriously. I get it. Rituals matter. They keep us together, and, when everything is changing, we know at least Friday is coming and we'll eat the same thing, at the same table, with the same people. Some things never change, and thank God for that. Elliot is holding hands with Maggie, but it's Friday. I pushed a Picasso, but it's Friday. I just hung up on the person who can turn me in, but it's Friday. It's Friday, and my period is exactly two weeks late.

"Miiiriaaaam. It's getting cold."

I rub the ink off with the soap until it burns. The water feels good.

"Miriam, the sun!"

I check outside. I can still see some light through the trees.

"Miriam." Mom's voice is closer, outside the bathroom door. "We're waiting for you. What are you doing?"

When I open the door, with my hair all messed up and my eyes narrow and straight, Mom shoves a pack of matches in my palm.

"You do the blessing tonight," she says, in a manner so clear and strong it immediately makes me think of bronze.

Following her down the steps, I notice her ass is sort of getting flatter. I imagine yanking her belt loops the way a toddler might, to make her mad, to pull her close. But she turns around and offers her eyes, round and deep, and says:

"I haven't told your father yet."

Which part? Her voice suggests I did something worse today than make the bus wait. For a second I think maybe she knows, but that's impossible. Mom was working at her gallery. If she knew, she would've already forced me to go back and apologize, or called a friend to make me intern at the museum. I would have to read Picasso's biography. It would already be on my desk.

No. My mother thinks I escaped the tedium of a high school field trip to examine the work of a creative master, one of her masters. She has no idea what happened. She just wanted me to be on time, and she wants to light the candles before the sun sets.

Dad is standing behind his chair at the dinner table, his hands wrapped around the back, poised and eager to sit as soon as I say the blessing. The food is waiting on a tray shaped like a big olive leaf, a wedding present that comes out on Friday evening. I've been through the ritual countless times. Dad ruffles my hair and smiles. I close my eyes and picture the bread, the cup, the candle. Even Adam could do this by now, and his dad is a Quaker who believes Jerusalem should be shared.

Mom plants her eyes on my forehead and purses her lips

in expectation. She's made all our favorite dishes. My body wants to sleep. I just want to sleep. She runs the gold charm back and forth on the thin chain around her neck—my initials and my date of birth. I think of Paloma's gold fish necklace. This whole thing feels like a test. Even Dad suspects it.

Mom pushes the candle across the table and brings her hands toward her eyes to prompt me. *Barukh atah Adonai.* I remember the words like a summer hit on the radio, and before reciting the blessing, I notice Mom peeking through her fingers, a kid cheating at hide-and-go-seek, to check on me. Like I said, a test.

I light the match and then blow it out before it can reach my fingertip.

"Light it again," she says, her hands still in mid-air, mid-prayer.

"You do it, Mom. I don't remember how."

"Light it again, Miriam."

I put the matches down and look for Dad, whose eyebrows squint to read what's behind the tension. He lets me drown.

"I don't feel good, Mom."

She drops her hands. God can wait until I get a grip.

"I thought you felt fine."

"Yeah, I did … I do. I just don't want to do this right now. I just want to sit down and eat. I'm really tired. Can you do this, please?"

"That sounds reasonable." Dad jumps in like a tiger through a hoop of fire.

Mom's shoulders assume position. This is familiar.

*You may have your ice cream when you've finished your peas. You may watch TV when you've cleaned up your toys. You may go to Adam's when you've done the dishes. You may walk home alone when you know how to punch. You may use my Leica camera when you graduate from college. You may sleep with someone when you are ready to be with them. And always use protection.*

Protection from what?

Dad lets out a weak sigh.

"I will say the blessing when you've lit the candle," she says.

I roll my eyes.

"Sarah . . . " Dad says, his eyes begging.

"Seth?" she says.

"Maybe we can try again next Friday," he tries.

"It's not that hard, Seth. I've cooked an entire meal. She can light a candle."

"I know, Sarah, it's great. Everything looks great. Let's just say the blessing and enjoy it. I'll say it."

"You can't say it, remember? Only the women, it's tradition. Right, Mom?"

My voice comes out whinier than I intended, a kind of silly, entitled whine.

"Light it, Miriam." Her final words.

I strike a match against the box, wait a few seconds until the flame is getting close, then drop it in my plate. Mom actually gasps. Before the flame can turn blue, I cover my eyes and say the blessing, for the bread, for the cup, for the Jews. Then I push my chair in and walk upstairs to my room, unable to shake the rage that has swallowed my head since Elliot told me he just didn't know.

*I don't know, Miriam. I don't know if I'm in love with you.*

As I dive onto the bed, I hope Dad is lighting the candles after all, that Mom is lifting the towel off the bread, and that he is devouring her delicious feast. To hell with me. It's not her fault I'm not as strong as she is, is it?

It's not her fault, it's not her fault, it's not her fault.

# FIVE

The *mal de mer* wakes me up. Mr. Wallace's ghost is silent and limp across the street. Next to my bed, there's a tray with some bread and a plate of leftovers, but I'm too nauseated to reach for it. I check my underwear. Clean. I tiptoe to the bathroom and try with the toilet paper. Nothing. I know I won't fall back asleep, so I do what I've done almost every night since the thought first occurred. I button my jeans, pull my hair into a messy bun, and I scan my room for his socks. Dark gray, slightly worn on the big toe, they smell like a basketball game. I've learned to roll them up so they don't bunch in my shoes. I'm a women's eight, Elliot a man's eleven. He forgot them here the last time we slept together, at the end of the summer, just before school started. *That* time.

When I bend down to tie my shoelaces, it feels like I'm on a hellish plane ride. The challah beckons, so I take a bite, hoping it will ease the sudden motion sickness. I brush my teeth twice, swishing and spitting furiously. My face is pale, and the freckles across my nose are graying. I have a crooked mouth.

I have two cameras to choose from: Lauren, the film camera (named after Lauren Bacall) and Bogart, the digital one, after her true love. They (the actors) met on the set of one of Dad's favorite movies, *To Have or Have Not*, second only to the legendary *To Kill a Mockingbird*, and that is only because Dad wants to be Atticus Finch. We used to watch these old movies together, when Mom was out late or in New York for a show. I liked to practice looking over my shoulder, lighting someone's imaginary cigarette, talking out the side of my mouth with that sultry voice. They barely even kiss in that movie, but Lauren Bacall taught me more about sex than sex itself. After watching the movie together, Elliot once told me I looked like her. Of course he did. I think that's when I gave in.

I walk past my parents' bedroom. Their door is open. His snores and her breath are warming up the hallway. I feel guilty, but I don't know what else to do. They're good parents. I'm just so tired. And, for better or worse, I can't sleep until I go out there.

While checking Bogart for juice, I think about the Picasso. The questions keep coming. Is the sculpture back up? Is it in the basement of the museum, where they keep the broken or ugly pieces? Do they have clinics for wounded art? I imagine a forensic scientist wearing goggles, brushing her hand across the sculpture's swollen belly, trying to determine how it happened. Who did this? Why? I check my recent calls: 240-667-8900. Is your light on tonight?

The bike rests against the back wall, and despite my general unease when I push the pedal, it does not disappoint. The tires are full and the breeze washes over the nausea. The first stop is Adam's house, but it doesn't count because I never really stop. I just have to go around the cul-de-sac and touch the mailbox with my right hand, like a trigger. It's a sad compulsion. The first time I went out at night, I came here but the lights were off. Adam's room faces the backyard. I didn't really want to see him. I just didn't want to betray him. Going out to take pictures is the sort of thing we used to do together. So, every time I go now, I pass by and touch the box, and sometimes I imagine it's a switch and that's how the lights come on. That's when I light up a house somewhere in Northwest DC, and all I have to do is find it.

Wisconsin and Connecticut, the main street arteries, are forbidden. It's too easy to find something there. It has to be a house. People have to live there. People who are sleeping, people who forgot to turn off all the lights, people who are too scared to turn off all the lights.

My tires cut the dry leaf piles on the back roads toward Chevy Chase. It hasn't rained in three weeks, and my feet itch like mad in these nasty socks. The oaks out here are enormous. I see nothing but street lamps so far. It must be past one. I've noticed the darkest hours are between one and four.

There. On the next block, left side, three houses up—a light is on. My guess is it's a living room, maybe dining. I stop the bike across the street. Before setting up, I check the houses around me. The rest of the block is lights out. Nobody is making secret phone calls in their parked cars. All the retrievers are snoozing in their monogrammed beds.

I forgot my tripod, which has never happened, but then again I've never knocked over a sculpture or deliberately messed with Shabbat, so this could be the new me, going bad like a child star on house arrest. I look for something flat to set the camera on, but the front garden has pretty stone walls that are too uneven to work with. I could try the roof of a station wagon, but I'm afraid the little red light flashing inside may be an alarm. The ground will have to do.

I take a composition book out of my trusted tote to even out the grass. The camera lens is wide open, like on a dentist's recliner. I check again. It's definitely a living room.

I make like a Navy Seal and lie perfectly still. My heart is finally beating, the way it does right when I'm about to take a picture. I Zen up and ignore the bed of acorns poking me everywhere.

It's perfect. There are bookshelves in the back, a coffee mug, a sweater draped on the arm of a green sofa. It takes forever for the lens to shut; my favorite kind of wait, when you can hear the light churning in there.

When I get back on the bike, I'm something close to happy. But happy is a ripple that hits land pretty fast these days and, after the first hill, I'm already thinking about him. I'm remembering my hair on his chin and him blowing it away. He just stared afterwards, right into my face.

Neither one of us could bear to move. He was wearing a gray shirt that smelled like us. I was wearing a red button-down I stole from my dad's closet. At least three buttons were undone.

You could see whatever you wanted, if you were looking, and he was definitely looking. I felt brave. His arm was sprawled across my waist. I looked down at his toes, then the creases of the sheets, then a strand of my dark hair again—a little mischief, a little pride. The whole thing felt so big and so little at the same time, like it could never really leave the room, like it would always be between the two of us. I was awake and asleep; contained and in pieces. Whoever says sex is nothing hasn't had sex with somebody who stared at their face.

A drop of something warm dribbles down my chin. I take one hand off the handlebar to touch it. It's blood. My lips are cut. I've been biting down on the memory.

I wonder what I could offer this ghost, what I could do to make it go away. I already painted over my walls. I throw up. I don't sleep. I lie. I yell at my mother. I ignore my best friend. I push innocent sculptures. I used to make things. Now I just destroy them. Maybe I could bike to 18th Street and pay twenty bucks for fake sorcery, some kind of exorcism, somebody who will tell me to put garlic in my pillow and a pound of sugar under my bed. What do you want, Elliot? You happened. You left. Now stop happening.

A block or so before my own home, I take out my phone to try Paloma's number again, but it looks like she beat me to it.

IS THIS MAGGIE? her text reads.

I type No and ride back to bed.

# SIX

I'm going to look for her black hair. My bike is parked against the wall of the Bishop's Garden, where I hope nobody will steal it. These are church grounds, after all, and I'm supposed to have a little faith. The gardeners have left the hydrangea heads on, like skeletons of summer. In the sun it's still warm, so I take my jacket off, wrap it around my waist, and walk inside the garden. We used to come here all the time when I was little, and I wish I was here to count carp in the koi pond. Boxwoods line the path right and left, smelling like dust and new earth.

A woman with huge shears trims the hedges. She's not wearing gloves, and the skin on her hands is a thin map of freckles and veins. The roses look embarrassed behind her; they're all chopped stubs with the occasional thorn.

I used to know this place pretty well, but I haven't been here in years. I walk past the empty gazebo onto a wide lawn.

This is where we'd have the occasional picnic, or toss a ball with my dad. I try to remember when exactly we stopped doing all that. I haven't caught a ball in years, I think, just for the sake of it, to see if I can, to feel that kind of surprise.

My watch says it's almost time, so I head for the side doors of the cathedral. Walking up the steps reminds me of running from the sculpture, and I consider how maybe you can get away with something but how stupid to think you can get away *from* it. It's Sunday, two full days after I pushed the sculpture, and my hands still tremble when I think of it.

Paloma picked the right place for her mystery. There are only a handful of people wandering around inside the cathedral, and a dozen more whispering prayers in the pews. Most of the morning worshippers have made their way back to their corners of the city. Senators find the time to cut their grandkids' pancakes while polite ladies wipe the bacon grease off their lips and the choir debates over next week's hymns. Christian or not, we all succumb to Sunday's tune: the promise of the morning, the sad afternoon.

The church itself is as impressive as I remembered it. Once in a while, when we used to come to the gardens to play, I got to go inside, but I had to be really quiet. I remember holding my breath, because I thought that was the only way to be totally silent. I was not allowed to touch the water—it's holy—and we could not be blessed in this place. We were only here to look and, maybe, think. This is a place people come to reflect. This is a place for repentance. Like I said, Paloma chose well.

The afternoons are getting shorter, so the sun has already

lit the stained glass on fire. Men, sheep, crosses, constellations—all the stories and symbols come out at once, and the cautionary tales share the light with the miracles. It's hard to look away. I settle into a pew near a stone column and wait. I reach out my hand to touch it, and it feels cold and smooth.

"Can't keep your hands to yourself, huh?" Her voice startles me.

Paloma, or whatever her real name is, slides next to me and smiles. She's wearing the same clothes she was wearing at the Air and Space, white T-shirt and jeans. She must be cold. Her hair is up today, so her cheekbones stand out more. There's something ancient about her face. I don't mean that she looks old, more like the lines and bones haven't softened over generations as they have with most of us. She looks like she belongs in an old photograph, like she comes from some unmistakable place. Her face is too strong to just be pretty.

"Hi," I say, worried I've been staring too long.

"Hang on a second," she says, as she lifts a huge bag onto her lap and loses half her arm in it, pulling out every item and setting it on the bench. A pack of baby wipes, a pair of sunglasses, a bunched-up scarf, a bursting wallet, broken crayons, a thousand paper napkins, keys, a rubber tiger, and a book. Maybe she babysits. The book is a poetry paperback, lots of cracks in the cover. It's obviously been used plenty. It's called *Twenty Love Poems and a Song of Despair*, by Pablo Neruda, translated by W. S. Merwin. She puts everything back in except for her phone and the book, which she keeps on her lap. I try to forget about last night's text.

"Have you read him?" she says.

I shake my head.

"Really? They don't make you read this at Sterling?"

"No."

The fact she knows my school still bothers me. It reminds me of her power.

"What do you read over there? Shakespeare, Yeats, Donne, Frost, Poe, Blake, Eliot, maybe a few of the Beats if you get a teacher who's a real rebel? No girls, I bet. Maybe Emily Dickinson."

I try not to let on that she's sort of right. I remember at least three of those guys from last year, and the only poetry book I actually own is an Emily Dickinson anthology.

"Don't get me wrong," she says. "I do like some of those guys. The realistic Yeats is heartbreaking, and no one can do sadness and space like Emily. I'm just surprised they didn't give you at least one Neruda. He's the easiest brown guy to include." She says "Neruda" like she speaks Spanish.

Paloma fiddles with her hair and ends up locking it in the same clip she started with. I notice a tattoo on the nape of her neck. It looks like a date: 6/10/11. She catches me looking and turns her head.

"Anyway, he's great," she says. "Not my all time favorite, but he's up there. Do you read any poetry?"

I shrug. "Not much."

"You can borrow it." She hands me the book. "Give it back to me the next time."

*What next time?* I think. What exactly does she have in mind?

"Thanks for coming," Paloma says.

"Right," I say. "I wasn't going to come. At first."

She nods and looks up at the flags draped over our heads, one for each state.

"That makes sense," she says. "I know this is a little strange. I didn't mean to scare you the other day."

"You didn't scare me," I say.

"Good," she says. "I just wanted you to know right away."

I nod, but she doesn't finish her sentence. "Know what?" I ask, whispering.

"That I saw what you did."

I take a breath and change course. "So why did you want to see me?"

"You go to Sterling, right?"

I don't answer. I go to Sterling. We've been over this.

"That's a good school, right? Do you like it?"

"It's a good school," I say.

"Your grades are good?"

"Pretty good," I say.

"You've got a nice family?"

"Yes," I say, wondering if she already knows something about them, wondering where she's going with this.

"So, why would a girl with a nice family, a good school, and decent grades decide to push a Picasso and run away?"

I don't know what to say. I have no idea where to start, or whether I want to answer at all. I stay quiet.

"Did you tell anybody else?" she asks.

I shake my head.

"You just walked away," she whispers, almost to herself, as if she's dreaming of something with potential.

Her Neruda book is still in my hand, so I open it up because I'm tired of sitting still while she thinks of what she can do with me. I read to myself: *"So that you will hear me / my words / sometimes grow thin…"*

Feeling Paloma's eyes on me, I carry on and read every word until the end. It all seems to speed up in the middle and take me along with it: *"You occupy everything, you occupy everything."*

I turn that line over and over in my head, and the words ring so true I realize maybe I've been hungry for them, in a way that night pictures, or music, or gray Atlantic Ocean walls cannot satisfy. Paloma smiles.

"You like it, huh? It's called 'So That You Will Hear Me.' It's a good one. It's better in Spanish though."

She takes the book from my hand and points to the opposite page, where the original poem is written.

"Like this part," she says, pointing to a new line. "In English, it makes no sense. In Spanish, it's different. It's more, you know, strong. Every word is stronger. *Now. Want. Hear.* It sounds so weak in English, but in Spanish it has force. It's like this. Let me try to translate. It's like, *Now I want these words to say what I really really mean so that you can hear me the way I want you to hear me.* Shit. I guess that's the same," she says. "Maybe you can't do it in English."

A woman in a purple robe shushes us. Paloma covers her mouth, but I can see her eyes laughing. I want to laugh too. She raises her eyebrows and gives me back the book.

"So, they're going to start playing the organ soon and we should really shut up then," she says.

I nod.

"You want to know the reason I know about the organ?"

"Sure," I say, because I want all the clues I can get.

"My mom used to bring me here on Sundays sometimes, for the rehearsals. She loved all kinds of music, but she always said the organ was the most serious instrument out there, and we should listen to it so we can feel close to God. Plus it's free. We'd take the bus from home and sit on the side where no one could see us, because she was always afraid. I don't know what she was scared of. Maybe those guys … " she says as she points to the purple-robe ladies. "Anyway, we didn't go to Mass, but we came here. We loved it. We would just sit super-quiet and listen."

Rituals. I think of my own mom at home, of how I can't possibly tell her what I did. Paloma's mother loved music like my mother loves art. It's like I smashed an organ. At church. I could smoke a thousand cigarettes, get drunk every Saturday, screw boys right and left, but this will really break my mother's heart. She's going to think it's her fault. She's going to think I was messing with her, that I pushed the statue just to hurt her.

"So," Paloma says, "let's talk. You know I followed you into the museum … "

"Right," I say.

" … and you' re not going to tell me why you pushed the sculpture. At least not now."

"I don't really know … "

"That's okay. We have time. The thing is, I'm in trouble. I have been for a while, and when I saw you push the Picasso, well, I knew you were in trouble too. After you ran, I went down there to look at the sculpture. Everyone was freaking out, but nobody seemed to know what happened. Nobody was looking for you. I couldn't believe it. Then I saw you on the stairs, and started thinking maybe I was the only one who saw. That's why I followed you."

"Because you saw me or because you're in trouble?"

"Both."

"What kind of trouble?" I ask.

"My kind of trouble," she says.

"Got it," I say.

"I had to leave the house," she says.

"Oh," I say.

"My mom got sick, and it was too much."

"I'm sorry," I say.

She nods. "She moved us all in with her brother and my aunt, but I couldn't take it anymore. Not right now. I had to go for a few days."

"You left?"

"Yeah, sort of. I just had to go."

"How long have you been gone?" I ask.

Paloma looks at me, but she doesn't answer. A few, long, cold seconds go by.

"So what do you want me to do?" I ask.

"I'm not sure how this is gonna work," she says, thinking, as she bites her fingernails one by one and spits them in her palm. I try not to stare and wait.

"I have a little brother," she says, louder than I expected.

"Okay?" I nudge.

"He's little. He's only four. My aunt and uncle have to work, and I don't know who's taking care of him." She stuffs her fingernails into the pocket of her jeans.

"Isn't your mom there?" I ask.

"I told you," she says, "my mom is sick. She can't take care of anybody."

"Okay. Well, is he in school, or is four too little? I don't—"

"Yes, he's in school," Paloma interrupts, "but I usually take him there, and tomorrow's Monday, and I don't think I'm going back."

"Ever?"

"I don't know. I don't know."

"Well, I'm sure your uncle will figure it out, and won't you—"

"Just be quiet for a second," she snaps, cupping her ears and squeezing her eyes shut. "I can't think. Let me think."

I shut my lips and think about what to do. Although she's already blackmailed me and snapped at me, I feel the urge to comfort her. Something about this girl and her trouble, whatever it may be, is pulling me in. I try not to look at her as she thinks.

"You said you haven't told anybody about the sculpture, right?" she asks.

"I don't think I said that," I whisper.

She smirks. "Yes you did."

I shake my head.

"You did. And anyway, you wouldn't be here if you had told someone. You'd be getting a job, or doing time, or begging somebody for forgiveness, because that thing was on the ground the last time I saw it, and they don't retire Picassos for nothing."

The tone has definitely shifted.

"What do you want?" I ask. "Why did you ask me to come here?"

"I want someone to check on him while I'm out."

"Your brother?"

"Yes, my brother. I need to make sure he's coming back home every day, after school."

"Is he in danger or something?"

"I don't think so. Not as long as he's home."

"Where else would he be?" I ask.

"Don't worry about that. I just need to see him. I just need to make sure."

"Why don't you call or something?"

"I can't call. They'll tell me to come back, and I can't go back there right now."

"But they know where you are? Right?"

Silence.

"They don't?"

More silence.

"Shit. Did you run away?"

"Sort of. It doesn't matter. Look, let's focus, please. You ran away, and I saw you run away, and now I need you to check that my brother is coming home and leave me out of it. At least until I figure out what to do."

"How am I supposed to do that without telling them that I saw you? Won't they know when they see me? Won't they ask?"

"Nobody's going to see you. You cannot let anybody see you. And you're not talking to anybody."

"How am I supposed to check on your brother without talking to anybody?" I ask. "That's impossible."

"I'm sure you can figure it out. I knew it when I saw you at the museum. That's why I picked you and came after you."

She's acting like she's chosen me, like this is some sort of privilege. I look at her book on my lap. I want to give it back, but I'm afraid of what she might say.

"I have to leave," I say, reaching for my bag on the floor.

Paloma picks up her phone and dials a number. The phone rings in my bag. I let it ring twice before I dig for it. Paloma nods, like she wants me to pick it up. I send her to voicemail. She puts the phone down.

"I knew it was you last night," she says, smiling a little.

Shit.

"You don't have to make stuff up," she says. "I just need your help."

"I wasn't lying," I say. "My name isn't Maggie."

"Of course not," she says. "I didn't think a Maggie could push a Picasso."

And this is the moment when I start to like her. Neither of us knows what to do, so we sit quietly for a while until a loud, deep sound startles the room. This is what happens next.

As the music makes its way through the vaults, down

the aisle, under the pews into our side-by-side guts, I catch Paloma biting her lip. Nobody else is moving. Paloma pulls the kneeler down and starts to pray, with her head in her hands. Her neck is bent, and that date is shining under her black hair. I think about what Paloma's mom said about the organ. I don't know if it's God, but I do feel closer to something.

When the music is finished, she surfaces, and I can tell she's been crying. I don't know what to do. Her book is still on my lap.

"Are you going to go back home?" I ask.

She says she doesn't know, that she'll go when this is over. I don't want to ask what she means by that, and I have a feeling I will find out sooner or later anyway. I don't want to push it.

"I do have one idea," I say, and she looks at me, red eyes and all, her hope a slap in my face.

"Is it a house?" I ask.

"What?"

"Where your brother is staying. Is it a house or an apartment?"

"It's a townhouse," she says.

"Okay. I can't promise anything about your brother or your mom or about anything else, but I can take a picture, if you want. I can take a picture of your house and bring it back to you."

Paloma smiles. It doesn't seem fair I don't know her real name, but I guess she didn't ask for mine either. She digs a pen out of her bag, pulls my sleeves up again, and writes an address on my arm. I roll my eyes. She takes my hand and holds it.

"Thank you," she says.

"I can't guarantee I'll see him, you know?"

"Just bring me something, and I'll keep your secret. You can save your real name for the next time we meet."

# SEVEN

My house smells like bark when I walk in. Like the woods. Like oak. Mom and Dad will be home as soon as they can, my phone reminds me, can I please leave the front door open. I need to think.

I head to the darkroom downstairs, the one I inherited from my mother.

Her rules:

1. Only two people at once.

2. Clean up.

3. No snacks.

My rule: Silence.

Adam has some trouble with that one, but he's learned to settle once we walk through the black curtain.

"You dropped me, Miriam," Adam said once on the

way home from school, when I was deep into Elliot bliss. "You dropped yourself," he said.

At the time, I thought he was jealous, and I told him so.

He looked me straight in the eye and asked me when the last time I took a picture was.

I let him believe I had stopped, that pictures were an intimacy I only shared with my best friend. But I hadn't. I have hundreds of prints from that time, of hands and grins and profiles. Elliot reading. Elliot walking across the street to meet me. Elliot not exactly drunk at a party we left early. Elliot in the arboretum. Elliot sleeping. Elliot in an inside-out sweater. Elliot nervous on a fancy date. Elliot's bass against Elliot's chest. I have more than twenty pictures just of Elliot's unmade bed.

I took all of those pictures with Lauren, my film camera.

Most people have traded in the darkroom for computers and the latest ink-jets. I have no problem with the digital process. Thank God for Photoshop. I know how to give contrast to the glaring noon light, bring out the blue in a flag or the rust on a bike rack. I could take out your nose hair, make your eyes seem less tired, brush your teeth. I can spend hours playing with layers and colors and shapes on the computer until I see what I thought I saw when I pushed the button. I'm not a purist. Picasso turned faces into houses into cellos into women with asymmetrical eyebrows. Who am I to diss that?

But I never really got over dunking a piece of shiny paper in a bath and watching my memory come alive, grain by grain.

Mom showed me how to print. We started here, in the film room.

I step into the booth and shut every light out of my world. I have no idea what this corner of my house actually looks like. I have never seen the paint, the holes in the wall where my father yanked out the dryer before I was even born, whatever bugs might be swinging on the leftover lint. This place is pure darkness, and it always has been as far as I'm concerned. It's been years since my mother first pushed me in here to fumble with her camera, and my fingers now know the routine like a ballerina at the barre. Take the film out of the camera, hook it onto the tank, reel. I still have to take a deep breath after I come inside so my hands won't blow the film.

The first time I took Elliot in here, I guided his hands through the whole process, not a word said, barely a breath taken. When we came out, his eyes were fixed on my face.

*You really are a different person.*
*Different than what?*
*Different than me.*
*What do you mean?*
*Separate,* he said, *separate.*

I didn't know if I should be proud or scared.

Now this plastic tube is my only proof. I unravel the film and try to fit the square holes into the reel, counting the spikes silently with my fingers. I missed a few. I unravel and start again, careful not to ruin it.

Through the layers of carpet, I hear someone in the

entrance hall. The door closes. The shoes come off and hit the floor. I can't see my watch, but it must be almost dinner time.

I drop the film into a bed of dust and darkness, and get down on my knees to look for it. Crunch. My toes find the film, and when I pick it up, it coils around my index finger like a scared cellophane snake. I feel for the scissors and knock them off the counter, where they dangle back and forth on a string. I grab them and start counting the spikes again.

Winogrand didn't touch his negatives for years. He liked to let them age, to forget about them until he was ready to make a print. In time, he could trust his gut to tell him which pictures to develop. The ones he could remember were the only ones worth looking at, period. And so I hope it goes with me. If only I could slip into an archival quality folder and wait until enough has happened before I look back. In other words, other shit needs to happen before I know what to do. More has to pass before I know which parts matter.

I grab a few prints to examine upstairs. Mom is reading the newspaper in the kitchen, but she looks up as soon as I walk by.

"How was your day?" she says.

"Pretty good, thanks," I say, not stopping.

"Did you get some work done?" she asks.

"Work?" I ask.

"Yeah. Downstairs. You haven't been there in a while," she says.

"Yes I have," I say.

"Okay. Well, Adam came in. He's in your room ... "

"What? How long has he been there?" I shout from halfway up the stairs.

"I don't know. Maybe ten minutes. Do you guys want something to eat?"

"No, thanks. It's fine. I ate already," I say.

Adam is sitting against a wall in my ocean and playing with my camera, the one I take out every night, the one I plan to use for Paloma's picture. He's handled Bogart a million times, but right now I'm nervous he'll break it. I want to grab it from him. His thumb is turning the wheel, and I can't tell if he's looking through the night pictures or messing with the settings.

"Hey Meems! It's about time," he says, looking up and smiling.

"Hey. What are you doing here?"

I try to calm down. I remind myself that he doesn't know.

"Your parents let me in. I wanted to see if you'd print some old stuff, but then I found these. I like them. You should bring them to class."

"What are you doing with my camera?" I ask.

"One might ask you the same thing. What have *you* been up to?"

"Meaning?"

"These pictures. I've never seen them before. The shed is my favorite. Whose house is that?"

"I don't know, Adam, but don't you think you should call or something before you come in and look through my stuff?"

"Sorry. Of course. I get it now. You haven't looked at these yet. I shouldn't have touched them. I forgot they might be virgins. But you know you can't leave Bogart lying around. It's too tempting."

I have this rule with digital cameras. I have to wait until the card is full to look at any of the pictures. I do it to keep the stakes high. It makes me look before I snap.

"Can you put that down now?" I plead.

"Sure," he says.

Adam lets go of the camera and taps his fingers on the carpet. His long fingers could wrap around my neck. It's been so long since we've talked in this room, about our lives, that I've forgotten how to answer his questions. My belly feels warm, and my head gears up to convert the warmth into rage.

"So, you want to do something?" he asks.

Since the break-up, Adam has been trying to get us back into our old habits, and it's driving me a little nuts. We used to go out into the city with our cameras and shoot whatever we found. We'd look through my mom's old photo books and argue about the importance of composition and the virtues of natural light. When I started to spend all my weekends with Elliot, Adam stopped coming over. I don't know what he did that whole year. I don't know what anybody did. After the split, he showed up with a camera, and I told him I wasn't taking any new pictures, so we went to the darkroom. He said we could just print, and I knew at least we wouldn't have to talk in there. We stopped after a week, because I said I wanted to lay off the pictures for a while. Now he knows I wasn't entirely honest.

"I'm tired, Adam."

"Come on, Meem, you know you want to. I know you

were working downstairs. We can bring out the old film and see how bad we sucked. I won't say a word, I promise."

I don't know what to say. The worst part about being sad or lost or whatever the fuck I am is that everybody you love makes you a little angry. The more they try to show you the way out, the less you trust them, like they are trying to sneak into your heart, like they've all got a scalpel in their back pocket.

"I don't. Want. To. And you can't just come in here on random afternoons, unannounced."

"Did you just say *unannounced*?"

"Whatever, Adam. As I said, I'm tired. I just want to get out of these clothes and sleep."

"It doesn't look like you sleep … "

I pull my sweater over my head, and he looks down. It's been a while since someone cared if I took off my clothes.

"It's only my sweater," I say. "I'm not going to change in front of you."

Adam rubs his face and looks at me.

"I never know what you're going to do," he says, more serious than usual.

I sit on the bed and take off my socks. He starts to get up, which makes him look like a giant. He walks toward me, and I have to work hard not to look away, to stay still, for once. He takes my wrist in his hand and rubs his finger over Paloma's address.

"What's that?" he says.

"Nothing," I say.

"Everything is nothing for you lately, Meem." Still holding on to my wrist.

"Come on," I say, "that's a little dramatic."

"All right. Fair enough, then. No more questions. I propose we pick a bus line and take it to the last stop, see what the city can offer."

"Maybe another day."

"But the leaves are bright, the air is crisp, this room is depressing, and you've obviously been out already. I have some excellent weird music a girl recently gifted. I'll turn that on, and we will roam the streets as silent companions. My word."

"What girl?" I say.

"Not important," he answers, his hand still on his chest from the promise.

"The one with the huge … you know … " I say, cupping my hands.

"Not going anywhere near that," he says.

"Too bad for you," I say.

"Not going anywhere near the question, not the things," he clarifies.

"Oh … "

"Can we go now? Have I been sufficiently humiliated?" he asks.

"No," I answer. "I'm sorry. I'm not going."

"You're too smart for this, Meem," he insists. "You're the smartest girl I know."

"I don't know what you're talking about, Adam."

"Yes, yes you do. You're just being mysterious or something. Look at you, taking beautiful pictures of houses in the middle of the night, showing up late to the bus and telling me you got sick. Is this about that shit-face? Because he's fine right now. I guarantee you he's enjoying his day."

"Good," I say.

"Yeah, good, and what's your plan?"

I cross my arms, hiding the address. "My plan? I don't know, Adam. What's yours?"

"The same it's always been. To look at stuff around me, to let it in, to stay awake, ask questions, see the beauty and the pain and all that shit we used to talk about. Everything that makes us different."

"Well, watch out," I say.

"For what? Watch out for what?"

"All of that."

"I'm not scared of life, Meem, and you shouldn't let one sorry dude make you scared of it either."

I think of what Paloma said about me figuring it all out, how she picked me for a reason and she was sure I could help her. I pushed a Picasso, met with a runaway at the National Cathedral, and am now going to Columbia Heights to spy on her family. I'm not scared of life either.

"You haven't been the same, and I get it," he says. "I get that it's hard, but I miss you. Everybody misses you."

"I'm sorry. Tell everybody I'm sorry."

"That came out wrong." He shakes his head. "I didn't mean it like that."

"It's all right," I say. "You were just trying to make the words say what you want to say and make me hear them as you want me to hear them."

"What?" Adam looks confused.

"Nothing."

"No. Not nothing. What did you say?"

"It's nothing, Adam. It's from a poem."

"Oh," he whispers, examining my face for clues.

I find my sweater and put it back on.

"You're not going to explain anything, are you?" he asks.

"I'll see you tomorrow."

"Yeah."

I wait for him to leave.

"Can I ask you something?" he blurts.

He's still standing next to me.

"Sure."

"Did you tell your parents you went to the Winogrand?"

I hate lying to this guy. "Yes."

"Why did you do that?" he asks.

"I just didn't want to explain."

"But you didn't go, right? Because I didn't … "

"I didn't."

"Did you tell them about the sculpture?" he asks.

I swallow hard and feel my face warming up. He knows. He knows, he knows, he knows.

He looks worried. "Are you all right?"

"Yes."

"Because your mom didn't know about it, and she was really messed up when I told her."

"What'd you tell her?"

"That someone knocked it over, and they tried to blame the school, but nobody knows who it was."

"Oh," I say, relieved but terrified. This adds a whole new layer to the lie.

"She kept saying she didn't know why somebody would do that. You know how your mom is with her art. It's like someone stabbed her dog or something."

"Yeah."

"You don't have a dog."

"Nope."

He shrugs and turns toward the door. I'm not quite done.

"Hey Adam," I say before he can leave, "do you think it's a big deal to knock over a sculpture?"

"Well, it's a Picasso, but nobody stole it, and maybe it was falling apart in the first place."

"But you said that couldn't be."

"I did?"

"Yes? You said those things don't just fall over. You said it's impossible."

"Yeah, well, I could be wrong."

In theory, but he isn't. Someone saw me push it.

"Are you sure you're all right?" Adam asks.

I really do hate lying to this guy, so I walk past him without answering, toward my bathroom, and my hand brushes his leg on the way out. I turn on the shower and let the steam swallow me up. I run over our conversation many times before my neck relaxes under the hot water, then I draw a square on the glass and wipe it clear with my hands. I see tweezers, toothpaste, a cotton puff. Click. There's my picture. I can't help it. It's like breathing. Some people think in words, others in music. We think in stills.

I shave, to buy more time, and notice that my breasts seem bigger, almost swollen. I cup the right one in my hand and it feels sore. I poke the mole on my left one to compare: same. I lather enough jasmine shampoo to smell like an Indian wedding. Three times over. I'm going to have to make it up to Adam tomorrow. I'm also going to have to tell him about the Picasso. I can do it. He will understand. He'll help me out. He said my pictures were beautiful.

I wrap a towel around myself and realize I forgot to take my clean clothes in here. It's all right, I tell myself. It's only Adam.

Back in my room, he's gone, and I'm actually disappointed. I take off my towel and lie face down on the bed. *I miss you*, he said. The water drips from my hair, down the slope of my hips, to the bed. I think of Adam looking through my pictures. All the feeling in my legs rushes up to the tiny spot where my body touches the sheets, below my belly. I shift my weight onto one hip to ignore it, but the thought insists and I rub my body against the bed until it's too late and my fingers reach down between my thighs with great, hurried purpose to find a place where I'm forced to let go. When I lift my hot face from the pillow, I realize I'm not at all ashamed. Just hungry.

# EIGHT

YOU DO HAVE A CAMERA, RIGHT?

yes.

OK.

AND REMEMBER YOU CAN'T LET ANYBODY
SEE YOU.

i understand.

YOU SOUND ANNOYED.

i don't know what you mean.

YOU SOUND LIKE YOU'RE THE ONE DOING
ME A FAVOR.

just tired.

EVERYBODY'S TIRED. YOU AGREED.

i know. i'll let you know. i have a camera.

THIS IS NOT A GAME FOR ME.

me neither.

IT'S TOO IMPORTANT.

i understand.

GOOD. YOU DON'T. BUT GOOD.

# NINE

I wake up with a pair of headphones stuck to my face. My ears are killing me, and it takes me a minute to remember the music I was listening to. There was screaming and singing and guitar. There's a photograph on my belly, and the light is still on. I must've fallen asleep while looking at it. The picture is of Elliot on the Metro, on our way back from a show. He's looking down and smiling, as if he's shy but flattered. It's my favorite Elliot face.

Elliot loves music as much as I love photographs, maybe the way Paloma likes poetry and her mother likes the organ. He can't survive three hours without a song. He's been to a hundred shows. Wherever they would let in a kid, he was there.

The night of the picture, we'd gone to the 9:30 Club to see an Irish music man who sings like his heart is a boat in the middle of a storm. We were in the front, near the small stage, and I was too embarrassed to tell Elliot this was my first concert. My hair had been ruffled by plenty of painters and photographers, but no rock stars ever came to dinner at our house. I was trying to act cool, like I could hang with the crowd of people who'd come to see this guy sing. More and more people poured in, and Elliot took my hand and led me through the crowd to a good spot near the stage. He held my hand as we waited for the guy to come out. That's when Elliot put his chin on my shoulder and told me my life was about to change. Those were his words, not mine. *Your life is about to change*, he said. Because of one man, on stage, holding a guitar with a gaping hole.

So, the singer said a few words, and everybody laughed, and that's when he tuned his guitar and started singing, gentle and sad at first. Everybody got real quiet, and Elliot stood behind me and wrapped his arms around my waist and the guy got a little louder, and the room felt like it was rising, until he was actually screaming this song, but it was still a song, except it made so much noise, inside and outside.

Photographs don't make noise. They don't rise and fall like that. They don't fill the whole room and take over your insides. They just stand still and sometimes you have to squint to really see them. This was more like swimming. When the first song was over, I couldn't wait for the next one, but I also knew it would never feel like that again. I'll never forget that first song.

After the band left the stage, I looked at Elliot for the first time in hours, and he looked so incredibly happy, and

I wanted every single bit of him. I wanted to live in the middle of those waves, to have something to scream about, to really understand what made that man write songs.

When we got on the Metro, our ears were still ringing, and we had to shout to hear each other. People were looking at us. I remember thinking everybody else looked tired. Elliot kept shaking his head and talking about how great it was, how it was so much better live than on the record. He leaned over and spoke in my ear, so I would hear him. He explained that music was like a knife for him, something that cut through everything. Then he sat back up, and that's when I took the picture.

It's of Elliot's face after the show, but it's about me. It's about the way I was looking at him and trying to understand him.

I drop the print on the floor and try to fall asleep. It's late. It's been a long day. I kick the music off the bed, rearrange the blanket and read a poem from Paloma's book. Nothing helps. Fuck it. Do what you need to, Miriam.

Minutes later, I'm on the bike, crossing the city in the middle of the night, going much farther than I usually go. The hills are tough and gradual, but I'm so mad I can't even feel it. I start on the side of the street and end up in the middle, since no one is there to honk or run me over. It's a little scary, but mostly it's nice to be alone.

It's hard to explain, especially in the middle of the night after a really long day, but I think I get what Elliot meant when he said music was his knife. So, there's life, right?

There's breakfast, and your parents, and the landscape outside the bus window, and your friends, and the guy you buy your coffee from, and your house, with your room, and your things, and your street outside your window.

Let's say you even have love, maybe sex, definitely fear. You're cruising—with your fair share of surprises and interruptions, but you're still cruising. Even when you get hurt, or when you are totally triumphant, you are sort of cruising, because the story is rolling, and you're in the middle of it, and it still makes sense. You're on the surface of your life. You are moving.

But sometimes, some days, some moments, something different happens. It doesn't have to be big. In fact, most of the time, it's not. Most of the time, it's a lady with a red coat who's crossing the street, and you can't take your eyes off of her. Or your mom undoes her hair, and it makes you want to cry. Or a dog runs toward you at full speed and you can't move, and you think he's going to rip into you, but you just stand still and he stops right in front of your legs.

Those moments are the knife. You don't know why, but things feel so clear and pure and real, you know it must mean something big, but you don't know what. Actually, when you try to figure it out, everything recedes and gets foggy, and you start moving again. That's why you need a knife. Once in a while, we all need to cut through the layers and access that place. Even if it means riding your bike across the nation's capital in the middle of the night to take a picture of a stranger's house.

Paloma's street is off a main road in Columbia Heights, where the buses have already stopped running for the night. There are only a few tired men coming home, maybe from work, walking under those bright store lights that make everybody look sick and yellow. Most people are in bed, including Paloma's little brother. But I can't sleep, so why not check the place out? She sounded antsy in her texts; maybe this will calm her down.

I get off my bike and walk it down the block. It's row houses. There are two street lamps, one at each end, so I'm relieved when I realize Paloma's house is in the middle, where it's a little darker and easier to hide. Thank God the whole block is asleep.

The house is three floors. A set of stairs leads up to a small concrete porch, where they crammed a rusty glider and a tricycle. There are bars on the first floor windows, and a basement apartment. I don't know what I'm supposed to look for, how I can make sure she knows I got the right house. On the top floor, I see a window covered in white spots. I use the camera to zoom in, and it looks like it's stickers, like the backs of dozens of stickers. This could be her brother's room.

I take a picture before I can stop myself, then ride back to my bed in one hurried breath.

Under the covers, a few hours left until morning, I think of a knife. I think of a knife making a clean cut, and I can see what's underneath, but it's hard to keep my eyes open. It's hard to look at what's inside. It's hard to be there for all of it. But I have to. Everybody has to. We all need a knife. Elliot's knife was music. I like to think my knife is photographs, but what I'm really scared of, what scares me most of all, is that maybe my knife was Elliot. And what am I supposed to do now? Go back to cruising?

# TEN

HEY, NOT MAGGIE! I DID SOME RESEARCH.

research?

PICASSO HAD FOUR CHILDREN.

ok.

BY THREE DIFFERENT WOMEN.

ok.

HE WAS A COMMUNIST.

oh.

LOTS OF HIS ART HAS BEEN STOLEN.

that sucks.

YOU ARE NOT ALONE.

i did not steal.

PARDON ME. DESTROYED.

HOW IS THAT PICTURE COMING?

I have it.

I KNEW IT.

# ELEVEN

"Go ahead and move those books, Miriam, so you can sit on the couch."

Ms. K's room looks out on the parking lot, where the seniors have written their last battle cries on their car windows in magic marker that won't wash out in the rain: Watch out, 2014. We've grown facial hair. We've had sex. We've walked home wasted. We have 357 Facebook friends. We know what motivated Othello and how many liters of water must be added to change the level of acidity. We're ready.

"Do you want any tea? I have some sugar in that closet," she says in a calm voice.

This is a new addition, the spa greeting. The last time I was in this office, I was a sophomore. I hadn't met Elliot yet, and I was still debating which AP classes would be most challenging, how we could sculpt my "edge." Mrs.

C, our previous counselor, was into edges. Ms. K, the new woman, is into tea, and I'm in no position to refuse.

I got called in here this morning during the last ten minutes of advisory, before classes start. I began to sweat when I got the note, and now I'm down to my last layer of clothes. Either Paloma packed it in and called the school, or the museum did. It's Monday—three days have passed since the field trip. It's about time someone figured it out. I should be grateful. This part will be over, and I can erase last night's picture.

"I only have green left. Is green tea all right?"

Sure. I look around the room for clues, something I can work with. There are no diplomas on the wall, no pictures of children in a silver frame, no knickknacks or itchy pennants. The only thing is a huge close-up of a forsythia bush, an explosion of thousands of bright yellow flowers.

Ms. K hands me the tea in a Styrofoam cup. It tastes like my front lawn. I sweeten it with two packs of sugar and keep the wrappers in my hand, unsure of how to get rid of them. I hope she gets to the point right away. I've had enough of mystery meetings.

"So, Miriam, how's it going?"

Obviously we're going to play some kind of game for a while. "Good" is a good-enough answer for now. I pick up a blue pillow my mom would buy and immediately put it back where I found it. My mom is going to erupt when she finds out. She's going to make me hold up that sculpture up for the rest of my life. I'm going to take out loans for the Picasso while everybody else goes to college.

"I called you in here so we could talk a little. Do you want to tell me what's on your mind?"

Ms. K stays quiet, which makes me extremely uncomfortable, which makes me sweat even more. Sipping my tea would help, but it's unbearably hot, so I just cup it in my hand and look around for a place to set it. Would Styrofoam stain the side table? Can I put cream in green tea? This is the stuff we need to know, what they should be teaching us in school. I take a breath. She seems serious about wanting to know what's on my mind.

"I'm just not sure what I'm supposed to say."

"Right," she answers patiently, like she's been trained. "You can start with anything you want. Do you know why you're here?"

I have some guesses, but I'm not quite ready to share them. I shrug.

"Do you have any questions?" she says.

Sure. For instance, who exactly called you and what did they say? Are you familiar with Picasso? Have you ever been to the organ rehearsal at the National Cathedral? Is your period always regular? Do you know Elliot?

"Where did you go to college?" I ask.

Ms. K looks a little surprised, but she quickly gets it together again.

"Maryland. University of Maryland. Not too far from here."

I comb through my mascot inventory, one of Dad's favorite car games.

"The tortoises?"

"Terrapins," she says.

She sips her tea, so I sip mine. I'm good at stalling.

Ms. K tells me about *the process* without really telling me what we're processing. I nod along, and she appreciates the gesture. It's pleasant and informative. She says she's spoken to my teachers, who all agree that I'm talented and smart. That's nice. I still don't know why I'm here, and I'm not about to ask. She has not mentioned a call from a woman named Paloma yet.

"So, Ms. D told me you were late to the bus on Friday..."

Ah-ha. I stay silent. I have a strategy, and I'm going to stick with it.

"She said you felt sick. Are you all right now?"

"Yes."

"I think she was worried when she couldn't reach you."

"I'm sorry. I should have called."

"She was a little overwhelmed that day."

Ms. K might be baiting me.

"Why's that?" I ask.

"Turns out it was nothing."

Now that's definitely bait. There's something she's keeping from me. We sit for a long time, long enough to feel uncomfortable, like I should move another pillow or something.

It becomes impossible not to speak.

"What did the other teachers say?" I ask.

She looks at me again, and again, she waits.

"You said you spoke to all my teachers..."

"Yes. That's right. Most of them said that last year you

had a bit of a dip in your grades, but you've pulled them back up," she says.

That I have.

"Some say you're quiet, a lot more reserved."

This cannot be enough reason to speak to a counselor. Ms. K is full of shit.

"Maybe I grew up," I say, shrugging.

"Maybe you did," she says, almost irritated but not yet.

"Do you have another degree?" I ask.

This time, she's not surprised at all.

"Yes," she says. "I have a Master's."

"In counseling?"

"No, social work."

"The Terrapeens."

"Terrapins. I got my Master's in New York."

Ms. K works at one of the most prestigious, progressive schools in DC. We don't wear uniforms. We have an amphitheater. We call our teachers by their last name initials, like in a futuristic novel. We have a vegan option at the cafeteria, a bottomless art budget, Black and Latino kids, gay kids, and kids with photographic memories. We all go to college, eventually. We're fine.

"Why did you move down here?" I ask.

"Why were you late to the bus on Friday?"

"Is that why you spoke to all my teachers? Is that why I'm here?"

"Why were you late?"

"I got sick."

Ms. K runs her hand through her short black hair and

pulls at her earring, smoothing the blue stone. Her rib cage moves up and then back down, taking her pink scoop-neck with it. Ms. K is very pretty when she's focused. She seems to be thinking hard, too hard for someone with the upper hand. Maybe she doesn't know after all.

"Anyway, I was saying … everybody says you hand in your work on time, but that you don't really participate."

I imagine what kind of kids Ms. K worked with before, in New York. Maybe those people actually needed her. I'm a brat who won't admit to a highbrow crime. She's got more important things to do. She looks young, maybe thirty. Doesn't she want to go back to where a difference makes a difference?

"Did you talk to the Yoga teacher?" I ask, hoping to push her enough that she'll get to the point, whatever it is.

She waits.

"Because I take Yoga once a week, in the freezing room. It's good to get different perspectives."

"Yes," she says, a hint of tension in her jaw. "I also talked with Mr. Green."

Mr. Green is my Photo teacher. He's the only one who deserves a full name.

"He said you take great pictures, that you're very talented."

The words sound like I fished for them, wet, dirty, flapping around for life. Why won't she get to the part where I'm bad? Why won't they talk about what makes me bad?

"He also said you haven't been showing at critique. He's afraid you are taking a break at the wrong time."

I reach for the rush I used to feel before critique, but

it's like trying to remember summer in the middle of a cold winter. Just the memory comes back, but none of the actual heat. I think of Mr. Green's gloomy office, that wall full of holes from the pictures we pinned up so that, one by one, they could be stripped of their mystery. We grilled each other every week. It was our own little search for truth. Every week we elbowed our way into each other's lives, looking for some kind of beauty. I used to look forward to that. Fuck you for bringing it up. Fuck Mr. Green for telling you that.

"I still take pictures," I say. "I'm just not showing."

"I know."

"I used to do it all the time."

"Yes, I know."

"And I'm still here."

Ms. K squints and stares, like she's lost an earring in my eyes. It's uncomfortable.

"I mean—I show up for class. I'm there. Why does he need me to get critiqued?"

"Well, I'm not sure, but I imagine he thinks you are good and you could be even better."

"Oh, I know I could be better. For sure."

"I mean really better. Good enough to go into fine arts, good enough to exhibit, maybe even good enough to make a life out of it. Like … uhm … like the photographer … Winogrand."

Now that's too much. The rising punk in me takes over. I stifle a laugh and she retreats, pulling back from her pep talk. She knows she tried too hard. She's hurt.

"A lot of students would love to hear that." She rights herself.

"I'm sorry," I say.

Now that we've established I'm not that student, I hope she gets to the point. Stop rubbing my lies in my face. Get to the part where I pushed the Picasso. Tell me why I did it and what you're going to do about it. But she won't help me. She just closes her notebook and sets it on the coffee table between us.

"Well, I'm here to help, and you can come in any time. We just wanted to check in to make sure that everything's okay. And everything seems to be okay."

In a fog of vague counselor terminology, I sense the meeting coming to an end, and I'm actually disappointed. Paloma obviously wimped out. That, or she really wants that picture, so she's willing to wait. In any case, no one here knows what happened. They all still think I got sick. At this point, even Winogrand would get a kick out of all this. But then why am I here? Why *the process*?

"We'll stay in touch," Ms. K says, offering to take my empty cup. I fight the urge to tear the cup into eight legs and hand her a Styrofoam spider, just so I can stay a little longer while she looks at it.

"So what do I do now?" I ask.

"Well, when you're ready, you can tell me the truth, and we'll be happy to help you out."

"The truth about what?"

"The truth about anything you want. Maybe why you're not taking pictures?"

"I am. I told you I was."

Then she tells me to come back in a week with five new photographs. She actually sounds pleased with her decision, so that's probably the closest to a punishment I'm going to get. Ms. K thinks this is an original idea.

"Any pictures?" I ask.

"As long as they're yours."

"Is this part of *the process*?" I ask.

"It's part of yours."

"Is this why you called me in here?"

"I called you in because we thought you could use a talk."

"Who's 'we'?"

"What?" she says, caught off guard.

"You said, 'we thought you could use a talk…'"

"Your parents called me."

Of course they did. They beat her to it. They probably talked to Adam and the whole dream team conspired to get me in here and get me happy, or whatever it is they miss about me. I get up and stuff the sugar paper in my back pocket.

"Miriam?"

"Yes."

"Did they not tell you?"

I shake my head. "Thanks for the talk, Ms. K. I'll do the assignment."

She gives me a wimpy smile and says she's looking forward to the pictures. I nod and walk out.

Adam is sitting on the steps outside the building. People are walking to and from class, their bags and hats and braids bouncing with every step. I think I see Elliot, but I'm wrong.

It's always someone else. This happens often. I walk past Adam.

"Hey," Adam says.

"Hey."

He jumps to his feet and, like his girl on Friday, hurries to catch up. I keep my head down and walk.

"I came to meet you so we could walk to Photo, and Ann told me you went to see Ms. K."

Ann. That's what her name is. Maybe they're together now. Adam would never tell me either way.

"How did Ann know that?" I say, not really expecting an answer.

"I have no idea. What were you doing in there?"

"I have no idea."

"Okay ... Did you bring your work?"

I roll my eyes. *My work.*

"The Green said ... "

"I know what he said, Adam. I was there last week."

"All right, Meem. Just asking."

He looks concerned again. He looks straight at me, and I feel a thousand little Anns staring at us, burning me with their envy. I've had this guy's attention since he was twelve. It's not my fault he turned out so good-looking. It's not my fault he's not a shithead like the rest of them. I didn't *make* him smile like that. I didn't give him that face.

"I don't have any work to show," I say, hoping that will stop him.

"Well, he said you could bring old work in. He said you could bring whatever."

"I know. I just don't have something … I just don't want to show."

"How about the pictures in your camera? The ones I saw at your place the other day?" he says.

I give him a disapproving look.

"What? They're good. They've got that thing the Green's always talking about."

"What's that?"

"You know. The hope and the fear. You know what I'm talking about. How there's only one feeling in the world and that's what everything's about?"

"That's two."

"What?"

"Hope and fear. That's two feelings right there."

Adam looks at me, smiles, and pulls my shoulders in close to his. There's the coffee smell again. And his detergent. The smell of his clothes, his house, our time together.

"Hand over the camera, Mardy Bum."

"What the hell is that?"

"Arctic Monkeys."

"Right. Too cool for me. As in Mardi Gras?"

"As in bummer. Let's have it. I'll show you what I mean."

The camera is in my bag. I took it just in case. I leave it in there.

"Come on, remember? You're my brave friend. You're the one who gets the best pictures. I always stop to think. You're the one who always goes for it."

"Goes for what?"

"Now you're fishing … "

"Fine. Whatever."

"Gimme Bogart and I'll show you."

"I don't have it," I lie.

He looks at my bag, then looks away. Then he puts his hand on top of my head, right in the middle where it's always cold. I keep my head as straight as possible until he takes it off. Neither one of us acknowledges this strange blessing. We walk the last few minutes without talking, just feeling the air between us shift.

"Okay ... " Adam says as we reach the arts building, a gray, pre-fabricated cube. "Wanna see something?" His eyes are the size of two, dark planets.

"Sure," I say.

"You can't tell anybody though. You have to promise."

I raise my right hand, my left one on my heart. Adam takes his camera out.

"Look," he says, pointing to the screen.

I frown. He knows my rule.

"Come on. Come on, come on, come on. It's not Bogart. It's my camera. You have my permission to look."

I lean over and hold my hand over the screen to block out the light. There she is. The sculpture. Lying on the ground. And my witness in her white shirt.

"Oh my God," I say, before I can take it back.

"I know, right? With the light on her face and all the feet around her. I wanted to get the guards—"

"How did you get this?" I ask.

"Fast. I was scared shitless. Ms. D was down there. That's her boots right there."

I did not expect this. Adam seems to be waiting for something, but it could be me making it up.

"It's perfect," I say quietly.

He smiles, blushes a little, takes the camera back.

"Are you showing that today?" I ask.

"No way. Not after I heard the museum dude blamed somebody in our class. I'm not crazy, like you."

I stop at the entrance and a cold, airless dread fills my chest. Adam holds the glass door open. I don't want to go in.

"After you," he says.

I shake my head again, and his face falls. He doesn't get it. "Miriam?" he says.

We walk inside, and I lean against the wall in the hallway. "What is it?" Adam asks.

"Nothing," I say. "I didn't eat very much this morning."

"You want me to get you something?" he asks.

"No, it's okay. Go ahead. I have something in my bag."

Adam reluctantly leaves, and I wait for him to be out of sight before walking back out through the glass doors. I take a long breath and find a place to sit, turning my face toward the sun. Second period just started. The campus is empty. Elliot is in American History, and Maggie is in Spanish. Because I'm pathetic and memorized their schedules, I know they don't have any classes together today. That means they'll have to meet by the oak tree, or the front doors where Elliot and I first spoke. I try to push those details out of my mind, to focus on the warmth on my nose and my cheeks and how it's burning my eyelids a little.

I still haven't gotten my period. It's now officially two

weeks and three days. I should probably take the test already. A girl can't spend her life waking up in the middle of the night and riding her bike until she's tired enough to fall back asleep, especially taking pictures of stranger's houses. It's going to get too cold for that soon. I'm going to have to come up with a better compulsion.

"Hey!"

I open my eyes again and look for where the noise came from. I can't see anybody.

"I'm right here, by the gates" she says, and I recognize the voice now.

Paloma is standing behind the gates of my school, waving for me to join her. I'm completely paralyzed. I can't decide if I should just ignore her, but then again she could scream "Picasso," over and over, until everyone walks out and stares. No school guard can keep a girl like that out. I walk over, checking behind me for any onlookers.

"Hi," I say. "What are you doing here?"

"Looking for you," she says.

"I'm at school," I whisper.

"Yeah, I know. Aren't you supposed to be in class?"

Right. "It's my break," I lie.

"Oh. Well. Do you want to take a walk? Do they let you do that here?"

"Yeah. I mean, it's probably better if I stay though. I have stuff to do."

"Okay. I just came by to see what it looks like. You have the picture, right?"

I give my creepy stalker friend the once over. She's

wearing the same thing, for the third time now. The jeans, the shirt, the gold fish necklace.

"Aren't you cold like that?" I say.

She shrugs. "You sure you don't want to go for a walk?"

"I have work."

But I feel sick lying to the one person who seems to know the truth. I resolve not to ever lie to this girl again. She could very well be my knife.

"I'm supposed to be in class," I say.

"What are you doing out here then?" she asks.

"Just thinking."

"About what?" she asks.

"Stuff I can't figure out," I say.

She nods and we both stand quietly for a minute, each on our side of the fence.

"Maybe I can help you" she says.

"I don't know," I say. "I'm starting to think it's just never going to be the same."

She laughs a little, not a mean laugh; more like a wise, tender laugh.

"Nothing is ever the same," she says.

I check for Bogart in my bag and consider showing her the picture I took last night, but instead I take out my green sweater, the one I was wearing at the museum. I hand it to her.

"I can't take that," she says.

"Go ahead," I say, "it's cold."

"Thanks." She pulls out the sleeves before slipping it on. It's tighter on Paloma than me, but I can tell she's grateful.

"How long have you been out here?" I ask.

"A while," she answers.

"I do have your picture," I say, "but can I show it to you later?"

Her eyes open wide. "After school," she says.

In my head, I run through all the people who could notice her, and then I remember Adam's picture of the statue. He would recognize her. He has that kind of memory, and she's his kind of girl, the kind he'd want a portrait of.

"Can we meet somewhere else?" I ask.

She narrows her eyes. I half expect her to grab my arm and write something on it, but instead she just names a time and place. I agree, and she walks away with my sweater on, looking both ways before crossing the street.

I turn around and find my spot in the sun, where I sit and realize there's nothing in my back pocket. That's where my phone was, so it must've fallen out in Ms. K's office.

I walk past the place where Elliot and I first spoke, and only when I'm on the other side do I notice I didn't hold my breath this time, like I have for the past month, to ward off the sentimental monsters. School. Here is the place where I spend my days. Here are the grown-up children, tucked in their boxes. Here are the teachers, checking the time. Here is Maggie. There is Elliot. Everywhere minds connect and disconnect, charting maps of thoughts all over the air. I cut through them deliberately.

Ms. K's door is open, but she isn't in there. I only have about ten minutes before the class period ends, and I need to find my phone. It isn't on her couch or under the pillows. I check back toward the door every two seconds. Maybe it's on her desk. Nope. There's a drawer with a lock and one without. I'm too nervous to open it. Back to the couch, lift the pillows, think of the last place I saw the thing.

When Ms. K says "Hey," I scream. A little scream. A yelp. She smiles.

"Oh my God, I'm sorry. You scared me, I was looking for—"

"Your phone?" she says.

"Yes?" I ask, hoping she'll give me a hint.

"Didn't Adam give it to you?

"Adam?"

She looks confused and moves away from the entrance, toward me. "I just took it to Photo, and he said you were in the bathroom."

I think like a liar: fast and stupid. "Oh yes, sorry, he did say something, and then we had to go and then I forgot to ask him again."

"Are you all right?" she says, her eyebrows all bunched.

"Yes," I say. "I'm sorry. I have to go."

"Okay. Are you sure?"

"Yes." And, before she can ask anything else, "I already took my first picture."

"Oh," she says, surprised. "That's great, Miriam, that's great."

I thank her again and head toward arts building, where I'm almost certain Adam is waiting with my phone and a few questions about where I've been.

I make a plan. If he asks why I skipped, I'll say I needed to be alone. If he insists, I will tell a half-truth, that I went to take pictures. He'll be annoyed I didn't invite him, but he'll understand that. He might even be proud. This is Adam.

The kids are starting to leave the buildings for lunch, and the noise goes in waves, lows and highs, screeches and whispers. I close my eyes and listen to it. I could pick out Elliot's voice if I wanted to. I open my eyes back up and feel a stabbing pain in my belly. I can't walk straight and I'm suddenly terrified, in front of all these people, in front of him, wherever he is. I fold and hunch my way over to the nearest steps, but the pain only gets sharper. Maybe it's a cramp, I think as I hear the voices and try not to make eye contact, praying that people have better things to do than notice me. Maybe it's finally a cramp. Maybe this is what it feels like when you skip a cycle and it comes back with a vengeance. They say your body can skip when you're sad. *They* can be right sometimes.

I try to breathe through the pain, but I can't. My body seems to be rejecting the air, spitting it back out into the light. I hop, still folded but filled with hope, to the nearest building and into the bathroom, where I manage to check and see nothing. White. Clean. The pain begs me to sit in a corner of the stall, so I do, and, as I hug my knees to my chest, I let out the air in a sad, short burst. It was gas. I rock back and forth until it's better, humbled by the needs of my body. I snicker. One minute, you're magnificent. The next, you're folded over by a fart.

I'm late. I run down the steps to the photo lab and slam the door open. A few guys look over and nod hello. They're busy examining their pictures. I've known them and their work for two years now, but they feel so far away. I'm surprised they even recognize me.

"Do you guys know where Adam is?" I ask.

"Try Mr. Green's office," Toby says, barely looking up from the screen.

Mr. Green's office is empty. This is where we meet for critique; a few photos are still pinned on the wall. I scroll over them (people, places, things, more people, no Picasso) and find I'd actually like to stop and look, but Paloma is pulling me away. Later. I don't have time.

Maybe I can find Adam's bag. He must be taking a break, grabbing a snack—he spends a lot of lunches in here. I search for his stuff under the stools, on the tables, in the hallway outside. I come back to the office and notice my phone on a side table. No message, no note; it hasn't even been turned on.

The thought does occur. The idea does strike. Maybe Paloma texted me when he had the phone. Maybe he read it. Maybe he knows. Maybe he turned it off so I wouldn't know he knows. But how. But no. But why.

I dial her number and she picks up immediately.

"Not Maggie?" she says.

"Yes," I say.

A pause, then, "Everything okay?"

"Yes," I say.

"Do you need anything?" she asks.

"What?"

"You called me," she says. "Do you need anything?"

"No."

A pause.

"I'm coming," I say.

"I know," she says.

# TWELVE

This is where Paloma wants to meet. Rock Creek Park—two thousand acres in the middle of the city. We need to meet before it gets dark. It's a long walk from the bus stop to the Nature Center. The trees here are mostly elms, hackberries, lindens. I know this because Elliot was a tree guy. He got it from his father, David.

David is an obsessive cyclist, one of those men who's too old to have so little body fat, the kind who only eats red meat on holidays and then bikes sixty miles in the frostbitten dawn to work it off. I spent months trying to forget his member struggling to pop out of those spandex shorts.

Elliot would go along some weekends, his pasty long legs sticking out of an old gym uniform and pedaling furiously to keep up with his dad. *I can't move today. We went to Rock Creek in the morning.* He whined about sore muscles, blisters, thigh burns, but never in front of his father.

The reward of a few hours alone with him, or a congratulatory pat on the shoulder, was always worth the pain. It was on these outings that Elliot learned about trees and birds, David being somewhat of an amateur naturalist. A robin has an orange belly; a cardinal has a red mohawk. The peach blooms before the cherry, and so on.

But Elliot never took me to Rock Creek. The last time we were in the woods together was this summer in Delaware. His parents have a house on Fenwick Island, and stayed there for almost a week. It was the end of June. Back then, I had no idea what an ovenbird was, but now I can't help but hear it call *teacher, teacher, teacher* from the forest floor.

"Why are you running away from me? Where are we going?"

Elliot's voice during our epic fight is still clear in my mind, not really as sound proper, but more as pictures of sound. A sharp whisper might be a rattlesnake. A sigh is a lion gone limp.

"You don't have to come with me," I remember saying, inhaling the pine all around us.

"Okay, can we just stop for a second? I can't think when I'm chasing after you."

"Don't chase. You can stop if you want, but I wanna walk. I want to get out of here."

"You don't know these woods. You're gonna get lost."

I could hear the ocean on the other end. I knew it couldn't be so hard to find the ocean. The salt air was already pulling at my skin.

"We've been here before, remember?" I say.

We had. Every day, at least once, we did it somewhere in the Delaware woods and then held hands and shut up until we got to the ocean, where he swam and I stayed afloat, hoping no sharks would smell our sins and swallow up my dream.

"Miriam, he's not a bad guy," Elliot said.

"No. Of course not. He's old and disappointed. My problem is you."

Elliot sighed. "What did I do?"

"Absolutely nothing," I said. "You just sat there, as if you had no opinion, as if nothing he said mattered at all."

"Does it?"

"Does it? Are you kidding me? Are you the same person who can't survive without music, who thinks a song is some sort of cosmic knife cutting through to the core of your existence? Are you the guy who plays three instruments and cries when we light the Shabbat candles?"

"What is that supposed to mean?"

"It means you do have faith and you don't think it's stupid. It means you believe that music matters, that photographs matter, that hope matters, that stories matter."

"So does my dad..."

"Maybe. Maybe once upon a time. But that's not what he was saying tonight."

Elliot rolls his eyes, which makes me want to push him over and kick him in the ribs.

"Were you there, Elliot?"

"Yes..."

"Let me remind you. We were talking about our plans, and he said he didn't think it was a real plan, that music and art don't save people's lives. I said I know music and art aren't antibiotics or surgery, but that sometimes that kind of thing can save a life."

"So..."

"So he told me it was time we stopped investing in things we can't count on, that it doesn't do any good. No, what did he say? I know: *It doesn't help anybody*."

"I know what he said," Elliot interjected.

"Do you? Because you were dead to the table..."

"What was I supposed to say?"

"I don't know, Elliot. Anything. That you think music matters, that it's why you spend your days immersed in it, that you don't think we should all just grow up and wake up to a world where the only things that count are the ones we can test in a lab, the ones that never ever fail us, the ones we have hard evidence for."

"I don't know what you mean."

"Don't you see that's what he was saying?"

"I don't know what you're talking about."

"He was telling us we should all be scared. That we should give up before we even start, that because God doesn't always give us what we want, we should turn away from everything that requires any faith."

We were both scared now, the ocean roaring ahead of us.

"Why are you even bringing God into this?" Elliot yelled.

"Because you can't count on *him*, can you?"

"I don't understand what you're saying," he said, which doubled me over.

"Yes you do," I said, tears in my eyes. "You understand.

You understand better than anybody else. I know you understand. You're just pretending you don't understand, because you're too much of a wimp to say you understand in front of your father."

"You need to chill out," he said.

"And you need to grow up," I said.

"You always act like everything is so complicated…"

Here, I could feel some kind of ugly truth coming on, and since nobody can turn away from ugly truths, I listened.

"Being with you is like…"

"What is it like?" I hissed.

"It's like you bring me down into this deep ocean, where I've never been before, and it's really beautiful, and it's exciting, but sometimes it's just too much…"

"I'm just too much?" I asked.

"It's just so intense. It's, like, sometimes you have to come up for air, you know, but it's, like, impossible to come back up to the surface with you."

"So you're tired? Is that what you are saying? That you're tired of me?"

"Can we just go back and sit down?" he pleaded.

"Do you agree with him?" I asked, desperate.

"Oh my God, please," he said.

"Do you think you'll wake up one day and no longer need your music? Or God? Or love? Do you think we're just wasting our time?"

"I have no idea, Miriam."

"Yes, for example. Miriam."

"What are you talking about?"

"Do you know who Miriam is?"

"No." He looked down and made circles in the sand with his feet, probably to stop himself from shoving me out of his way.

"She's the one who saved Moses, watched him float in a little basket down the river when the Pharaoh wanted to kill him."

"So what?" Elliot said, losing patience. "My father is the Pharaoh?"

"No."

"Oh, no, I'm the Pharaoh! I'm the Pharaoh!"

"You didn't answer my question," I said.

His eyes were green, green, green—like Oz green. "It was a stupid question."

"Oh, now you're calling me stupid."

"I didn't call you stupid," he said.

"No. You just think I'm too much."

"Miriam."

"Elliot?"

"It's one thing. He said ONE thing. You've been here for five days. You've gone on hikes with him. You've had dinners with him, and one time he says this thing and you totally write him off."

"Should I be grateful?"

"I'm not saying that."

"What are you saying?" I ask.

"I'm saying he's my father and maybe he's wrong, but I love him, and I still respect him."

He was trembling when he said that. I knew I could

make it to the ocean, but it could not be with Elliot. Elliot could go back to his Mommy and Daddy.

"Good." I nodded. "And I'm saying my grandfather took the last boat to America before the Nazis raided his house, and that's why I'm here to fuck you in your summer home. I'm saying my mother gave up everything and lived in a rathole for years, just so she could take photographs for the rest of her life. I'm saying that guy at the concert was your knife, and he probably saved your life, and now you're turning your back on him and everything he does. I'm saying we're in love, but it's nothing anybody can count on, but that doesn't mean I'm going to stop when I get tired. Faith isn't something we can just get rid of. We need it. Everything runs on it."

You could say we would've never broken up if it hadn't been for David's rant on the useless arts. Or if Elliot hadn't been so damn passive, so quiet. But what kept me shivering until I got home was the fear—not of David, whose comments I'd heard before; not of Elliot, who'd proven his loyalty enough other times—but of love itself, stretched from my Opa, through my mother, to my favorite second grade teacher, to the boy who kissed my breasts in the kitchen of his summer home after his parents had gone to sleep.

All I kept thinking about was his ocean metaphor. Maybe he was right. Maybe I was too intense, too tiring. Maybe it was easy to fall in love with me, but not so easy to be with me. Maybe that's who I was.

But what was I supposed to change then? How could I give in and not give up? How could I come out whole? What would have to die for me to stay close to Elliot, to anyone? Was it possible to be in love and be yourself? Love is loss is love is loss is love.

That day, I made it to the ocean and swam for an hour. When I got back to the house, they were all gone, maybe to look for me, maybe to get ice cream. I left a note for Elliot and took a cab to the train station, where I bought a ticket for the first train back home. That's where I took the last picture of the summer. From that train, of a street in the Wilmington ghetto.

I'm in your woods, Elliot. Can you hear me? Picasso's daughter wants to meet me in your woods.

# THIRTEEN

I pass the empty picnic areas and walk up the hill to the Nature Center, a small building that reminds me of a mountain lodge. Paloma is sitting on a bench outside the entrance, her big bag between her knees. She looks disappointed.

"It's closed," she says.

"Oh."

"I should have remembered. It's closed on Mondays."

"What's in there?" I ask.

"Let's see if I remember. There's a bookstore, a play room, and even a planetarium for people interested in stars." She winks at me and smirks. Her favorite part seems to be the taxidermy: "They have an owl, a fox and a whole raccoon family, all stuffed up …"

"How do you know this place?" I ask.

"My mom used to take me here," she says.

I try to imagine her mom and what she might look like. I'm afraid to ask about her illness.

"Your mom sounds pretty cool, you know, taking you to the Cathedral and the Nature Center," I say, trying to sound casual.

"She took me everywhere. I don't know how she found out about these things, but she knew this city better than people who've lived here their whole lives. She was incredible," Paloma says, her eyes a little watery.

"I've never been here," I say, "and I've lived here forever."

"My brother loved to feed the snake," she says. "You can watch a ranger feed a rat to the snakes."

"No thank you," I say. "Like a live rat?"

"Yup," she says. "They strangle it, swallow it up, and then they sit there for days, depending on how big the rat is."

I shudder.

"What?" She laughs. "You don't like rats?"

"Not so much," I say. "I especially don't like rats being swallowed by snakes."

She smiles. "My little guy would go right up and touch it."

"You mean your brother?"

She looks defensive. "Yeah," she says.

"What's his name?" I ask.

"Pablo."

"Like Pablo Neruda," I say.

"Yeah," she says. "He was my mom's favorite poet."

I look for the book in my bag, but I left it at home on

my unmade bed. I tell her I forgot it, but she doesn't seem worried.

"Do you want to show me the picture?" she asks.

I show her which buttons to press and hand her the camera. I stay standing. It's my only leverage.

She looks at the screen for an eternity. Her eyes squint, as if she wants to see what's beyond the image, inside the machine. She rests the camera on her lap and unties her hair. A few strands get caught in the elastic. She keeps her eye on Bogart, braids her hair, and picks the camera back up. She moves it closer to her face, occasionally pressing buttons without making any comments.

I have no idea what she's thinking or whether she'll be satisfied. I did get the stickers in there, which must be her brother's room. And that's the door she'd walk through every day. Those are the windows she'd opened when the rooms need air. That's the brick. That's the glider. Those are the bars. That's the house; it's better than nothing.

Paloma asks me to look at something with her, and I tell her about my rule about not looking at the pictures on the screen.

"Well then, how would you know it's what I want?" she says.

"You mean, how do I know it's good?"

"Not exactly. I mean, how do you know you got it right?"

"This is your house, right?" I ask.

"My uncle's house."

"And I got the house."

"Not exactly."

I look at the photo, at the stickers. She looks closer and smiles a little.

"Those are his dinosaurs," she says. "He's only four, but he knows the names of all the dinosaurs."

Without looking up from the camera, she says she wants another picture, in the daylight, after school, when Pablo gets home.

"I told you I couldn't guarantee—"

"This doesn't prove my brother's all right. That's his room, but I don't know that he's in there. I don't know he's safe."

"Okay … "

"You have to get closer than that," she says, looking up now.

I try to argue that it's too dangerous, but she stands her ground and tells me we had a deal.

"You said to bring you something and you'd keep the secret," I say.

"I did. Now bring me something else. Something that proves he's in there."

"Well, how many pictures do I have to take?"

"As many as it takes."

"That's not what you said. That could be a lot of pictures. I could get in trouble."

"In trouble? Seriously? You're already in trouble."

"Well, so are you."

She starts thumbing through the pictures really fast. She's gonna break it if she keeps going like that.

"You're the one who offered to take pictures. You're the

one who went all the way across town to take the picture," she says, the wheel on my camera scanning through the photos at top speed.

"How do you know I live across town?" I ask.

"I don't know. I'm guessing you don't go to Sterling and live in Columbia Heights?"

I blush. I said I wouldn't lie, so I won't. "No. I don't live in Columbia Heights . . . "

"I didn't think so," she says.

" . . . but I don't know how many times I can do this."

"Let me ask you something," she says.

"Okay."

"Did you really think that this would be it? Did you think you would push a Picasso, take one picture for me, and then everything would be over and you'd go back to your life?"

I guess not. I don't know what I thought. I guess so.

"You have more than ten pictures of houses in here, and I presume they are not all your house. You took them at night, which means you're not sleeping very much. I'm only the most recent of your troubles. You had a problem before you met me. You can stop taking pictures if you want, but this is not the end, my friend."

"Are you going to tell somebody?" I ask.

Paloma shakes her head. She's annoyed. "What do you think?"

"I don't know," I say.

"Do you trust me?" she asks.

"I don't know," I say. "I think I want to, but I don't know."

She looks at me now. The screen gets tired of waiting and turns black.

"Why did you push the sculpture?"

"I guess I was mad," I say.

"About what?"

"About everything, I guess, but mostly about this guy."

"What did he do?"

"He turned out to be a wimp," I say.

"That can't be too surprising." She shrugs.

"Well, I was surprised."

"So you broke up with a wimp, and now you knock over precious art and take pictures in the middle of the night?"

"No. He left me, and yes, I pushed a sculpture, and I do take pictures in the middle of the night. It helps me to fall back asleep."

"That's a lot of grieving for someone with no balls," she says.

"Maybe," I say. I leave out the part about my period being late.

"What's the guy's name?" she asks.

I shake my head. "It doesn't matter."

"Names always matter. I just want to have a name I can match the asshole to," she says, just like that, which makes me smile.

"It doesn't matter," I repeat.

After a long moment and a sigh, she starts looking at the pictures again. I still haven't asked her why she came to school today.

"I just thought … "

"You wanna go? Go," she says, still looking at the pictures. "Who's keeping you? Go."

Her eyes are focused on the camera, but she won't stop pressing buttons long enough to really be looking. She's nervous. I don't know if I should snatch the camera from her hands and run. I go over the scenario in my head.

Here it is. I take the camera, I start running. I run through the woods, on the horse trail, down to the mill. I walk to the bus from there. I go home. Mom and Dad are there. They've spoken to Ms. K. They know I skipped class this afternoon. They ask me a million questions. I lie. They get sadder. I suffer through dinner. I try and fall asleep. I can't. I check my underwear. I go take a picture in the middle of the night. Then what? Then nothing. A whole bunch of nothing becoming something I cannot go back to erase. It hits me. She's not the one who has to let me go. I'm the one who has to let her go. And I can't, not yet. You know why? Because she sees something no one else can see. She picked me. She chose me, and I'm sure she will eventually tell me what this is all about.

"Do you promise me this is your uncle's house?" I ask.

"And not my former restraining-order boyfriend's?" she says.

"Yeah, not that," I say, not quite sure whether she's joking.

She stops scrolling through the pictures and looks me straight in the eyes. "I promise you it's the house."

I sit down next to her without looking at the screen.

She says she wants the picture soon. She reminds me that I shouldn't let anybody see me.

"But aren't they worried about you?" I ask.

Paloma sighs.

"If you want me to do this, you have to tell me a little bit more. You're going to have to explain a little bit more," I say.

She sighs again.

"It's hard to explain," she says, "but I will, as soon as I see them. I will. I just can't do it now. Sometimes we do things and we don't know why. Maybe the answer comes later."

I hope she's right. If I didn't think God was pissed at me, I would pray she's right.

"You still don't know why you pushed the statue, right?" she asks.

"No. Not really."

"But you want to know, right? You feel guilty?"

"Yes."

"So then we're exactly the same."

That last sentence stings. The thought sends an army of ants rushing underneath my skin. The thrill of recognition, the bite of truth—I know that from somewhere. I've buried that feeling.

Something rustles in the trees behind the building. Paloma gets up and walks down a wooden walkway, my camera still in her hand.

"You have to come look at this," she whispers, motioning for me to join her.

My feet feel light and nervous on the wood. Someone raked the leaves off to the side, and the ground below us is every shade of brown. We're on a lookout, a few feet above the worms. Paloma points to the woods, and I count one, two, three, four, five deer foraging in the forest in front of us, no more than fifteen feet away. Occasionally one of them looks up and chews, and a twig or a stem leaks out of their mouth, making them look extra helpless, those big glassy eyes saying nothing at all.

Paloma breathes.

"Wanna take a picture?" she says.

I take the camera back and look through the view-finder, past the deer, at a rock on a hill in the forest. It's hard to believe it will all grow back when spring comes around, hard to even want that. I take a picture, and I feel better, like I have a heart that works.

"My name is Eva," she says.

I look at her face, the fine wrinkles around her eyes, the almost-smile on her lips, a smile of quiet relief. It feels warm. I'm touched she finally told me something I can count on.

"Miriam," I answer.

She tells me next time she'd like a picture she can hold on to, one she can take with her. Then she's off, big bag and everything. I watch to see where she goes, but it's getting late and my parents are waiting for me. I'd like to tell my dad about this place. He'd like to see a snake swallow a rat. I look back at the deer and start walking away.

The thing with DC is that the woods are everywhere. Walk, bike, run, or drive no more than two miles in any direction and you can find enough green to lose yourself in. I mean, places where you could scream without anybody hearing you. Or bothering you. Or telling you to stop. Places where you can't hear the cars, where the ditzy deer barely look up at you, where the alligators used to hang before the White House was built.

I run down the walkway to where the dirt trail starts, to where it smells more rotten. Then I run some more, away from the deer and the building, panting, toward the top of the hill, to the highest point of the loop. When I get there, I'm sweating. From my rock, all I see are trees. I feel sort of free. I may not be done with Eva, or Picasso, but this feels free, as free as my bike, as free as the pictures. Fuck love. This is a hundred times better. I scream as loud as my voice will let me.

# FOURTEEN

All I want are pretzels, and all we have are wheat crackers. I make a mental note to ask Mom to buy me some chips, but that doesn't seem fair since I skipped classes, knocked over a sculpture, and regularly sneak out of our house in the middle of the night. I should buy my own damn chips. At least until I figure out what I'm doing.

Thank you God. Behind the cereal, a shiny Snyder bag with a few leftover nuggets beckons. Buttermilk Ranch, no less. I crunch through the sour/salt/sour and brush the crumbs off my teeth with my tongue. Shame on me for ever turning this junk down in the past. I have about half an hour before the first parent walks through the door, not enough time to bury the rush of my afternoon with Eva. I eat the whole bag.

I walk upstairs to put the camera in a safe place, but when I open the door, I see dozens of prints, floating like shiny rafts on my bedspread. I hesitate before walking any closer. It's strange to see my secret like this, exposed and on my bed. It seems too dangerous to touch. I count twenty-three prints from where I'm standing. There is no sound, but the pictures are deafening. It's as if my sleepless nights are all screaming at once.

I walk closer, hoping to shut them up. I remember taking most of them: the house with the ivy, the red cat sleeping on a kitchen island, the dinner table never cleared, the neon house number and the stained glass door, the bright tongues of tropical flowers in a crowded sunroom, the copies of *Foreign Policy* magazine turning a coffee table baby blue. The best of my night wanderings is here, impossible to ignore.

My first one, the shed, is on my pillow. I took that one on the first night of insomnia, when I started checking my underwear for traces of blood. The walls of the shed are green from a flood light. I remember that light. Behind the window, several empty bottles are lined up on a shelf, each one a little different, all darkened by the night. I pick the print up and see a note in the back. The handwriting is familiar:

*Come out in the light.*
*Adam*

I can feel the color leaving my face. I run to the bathroom and puke ranch dressing until my throat burns.

"Miriam!" my mother yells.

This is too much. Picasso, Paloma, Eva, Ms. K, Adam. I rinse my mouth and catch my breath. I want to look at the pictures one last time. There they are.

Adam. Adam who dunked a kid in the fish bowl over a camera our first year at Sterling. We had biology together, and one sweaty day he got into a fight with a bunch of guys who were messing with his camera. I was in the front of the room, drawing a nucleus or something, when I heard Adam getting worked up. *All right, dude. Okay, give it back. That's funny, give me the camera. Hey. You're gonna break it. Give me the camera, man.* His nerves revved the boys up, and they turned into a pack of drooling, dumb dogs. One of the zit-faced jackasses thought it would be funny to throw the camera in the class aquarium, so Adam returned the favor and shoved the kid's head so far into the water, I can still see the bubbles scattering the fat fishes.

The teacher had to pry Adam's fingers from the boy's neck long after the whole class was done gasping and hooting. I was the only one who understood the gravity of the crime—the camera had been our shared love from the start. He had to sit in the office for the rest of the day. I waited until everyone had cleared out to sit next to him, let him curse, get him a lemon Snapple, and wait for his mom to take us home. I lent him Lauren for five months until he had saved enough money for a new camera. He would have done the same for me.

Adam trusts me. Adam should know about the sculpture, and Eva, and whatever else I find out. Adam would care. He would understand. I think of yesterday. He must have taken my photos with one of those gadgets he's always plugging into his camera. Maybe while I was in the shower. I want to see him now, but Mom will never let me past her, not if she knows about me leaving school today.

"Miriam!" she yells again.

I do what they do in the movies, what I've dreamt of doing since I was nine years old and reading my mom's vintage Nancy Drew books. I open the window, step onto the sloped roof, and climb down the porch pole, scratching myself silly on the bare clematis. Once I'm on my street, I actually think through my choices. It's only four blocks, but my shoes are still inside. My mom knows I'm here. I can still taste the puke, and I'm really really thirsty. I brush my pants off and walk back through my front door. I will go after. When I'm done facing her wrath.

"Hey Miriam," Mom calls from the kitchen.

"Yes."

"Sit down in the living room please."

My mouth is sour and dry. I can't believe I climbed out the window. What if Mr. Wallace saw me? What if I had fallen off the roof? This last hypothetical is kind of hilarious, and I want to laugh, but my mother does not look like she's in the mood. I sit on my favorite corner of our old couch, squishing the printed birds and flowers. I get serious and gear up for a logical consequence, Mom's favorite kind.

"Ms. Kiper called me."

From the tone, I figure my mother had time to rehearse this confrontation, maybe in the car on the way back from the gallery. She wants to sit but she can't get comfortable, so she leans on the windowsill across from the coffee table. The hanging pot is level with her head and it looks sort of stupid, like it's been cut and pasted. I bite my tongue. Why is everything so absurd all of a sudden?

"Can I tell you what happened?" I offer.

She relaxes, but I don't, since I actually know what happened and I also know I can't tell her half of it. Her eyes are begging. She comes closer and I'm comforted by her smell, the same greasy flower face cream she's used ever since I can remember. Her smell. I think I made a mistake. Her shoulders come down, she is listening, patiently waiting. I have to talk before she does.

"Go ahead," she says, "tell me."

"I went in to see Ms. K, Ms. Kiper, and I felt sort of dumb, to be honest. She was nice and everything, but I didn't really know why I was there. I don't know why you guys didn't talk to me first."

My mother takes off a shiny red plastic bangle and turns it over in her hands, looking for balance and the right words.

"We didn't know *what* to do, Miriam. We wanted to check in, and we wanted to do it right. We didn't have time to tell you. We should've told you."

Okay. She doesn't know about me skipping. She was just checking in.

"Nothing's wrong with me," I say.

Mom sighs and puts her bangle back on.

"I know maybe nothing's wrong with you, but you haven't been talking to us, and you're pulling away from everybody else."

"You mean I haven't been nice to you. That's what you mean. Look, I'm sorry. And who's everybody else?"

"I'm not going to get into that. We just want to know

what's wrong. We're here to help, love. What can we do to help?"

This is the part she said out loud in the car, this is the line she had to make sure she delivered. Maybe Ms. K coached her.

"Help me do what?" I say.

She leans back again. "Okay, Miriam. You were late to the field trip bus, and I'm still not sure why because we both know it wasn't to see Winogrand. You barely eat, except for whatever junk is left over in the pantry. You don't talk..."

"How do you know I didn't go see Winogrand?"

We're both surprised at how loud my voice is. I'm sure now that I don't want her to know what happened. Not before I know why I haven't been bleeding. Not before I find out why Eva wants the pictures, why she's left home.

"Miriam, what are we supposed to do?"

Her words are so earnest, I don't know how to answer. There's no room for snark.

"I was mad, Mom. I was just mad. That's why I did the thing at dinner that night. Don't you ever make mistakes when you're mad?"

"All the time," she says. "All the time."

"Okay, then you don't need to jump in to rescue everybody all the time."

"What does that mean?"

"It means you always have to fix things."

She looks at me like she's trying to crack a code.

"What would you have me do?"

"I don't know...let me make mistakes."

That sounds vaguely right, so I repeat it.

Yeah.

"Let me make mistakes. Don't act like you never make them. Don't act like you can always fix everything."

Mom's eyes are turning red. She gets up and points a finger at my face:

"I am forty-four years old, Miriam. Don't talk to me like you know better. You know yours and I know mine, but I'm still your mother. That's what mothers do."

The words are coming out strained. She's fumbling.

"We'll talk about this later. Tomorrow, actually. With your father, in Ms. Kiper's office, after school."

"All right," I say, "fine. I guess we're officially in family therapy, like everybody else you know. As long as it *helps*."

She walks back toward her kitchen and stops to pick up my shoes, align them, and stick them under the bench. My elbow is still burning from the attempted escape. I lift my shirt and see a scrape above my hip. Adam's phone number runs through my head. The night pictures are still breathing on my bed.

Adam calls my mother Meema, as in Meem's Mama. *Meema, you have the longest hair I've ever seen. Meema, my mom said I can stay for dinner. Meema, tell us the story of when you met Lee Friedlander. Meema, how about putting our pictures up at the gallery? Meema, let me do the dishes. Meema, can we use your printing paper? Meema, this roast is amazing. What do you think of the Iraq war? Meema, what about the settlements? Where are the paper towels?* Years and years of riding in my car, eating my cereal, making my mother laugh. *Meema, is Miriam up there?*

You want me out in the light? Fine.

I tell Mom I'm not hungry and I'll be back in an hour. She tells me that's not the way it works, and I tell her I need to calm down, which are the exact words she's asked me to use since I was three. Mom is disarmed.

I'm so tired, but the bike is the place where I make the most sense. I push, and it goes. I circle around my neighborhood, feeling my gut grow full and my mind strangely empty. Here is my body, I think. Nice to meet you, I think. Where have you been, I think. Here is the cold air, the burn in my thighs when the hill starts. Here is my sweat. Out in the light, like you said.

I ride toward Adam's and stick my arm out to touch the mailbox without stopping. My fingers hit the metal, but they don't make any sound. A voice calls from the garage, and I pedal so fast I run the next three stop signs. I freeze in the middle of the next block, letting several cars roll by me before I remember where I am and what I was doing. Then I push away from our world, toward the place no one else knows about, the place where I feel awake.

I only make it halfway to Eva's before the hour is up. I'll have to turn back and try again tomorrow. I ride fast on the way back. Back in my part of the city, I ride past the pool where I learned how to swim. I ride past our shoe store, our movie theater, the post office where I got to stick the stamps. I ride through neighborhoods where people garden, and go to college, and have dinner parties where they talk about the election, whichever one is up next. My neighborhoods, where it's safe and relatively happy, where people shield themselves from grief until it hits them in the face. Because it does, for all of us.

I remember Mom's eyes, the effort they made to stay dry, the love in her self-control. I know she's worried, but I cannot leave my mystery girl now, with that sculpture off the pedestal and her house in my camera. For everyone else, I am a picture, a map of light. To Eva, I am the girl who was mad enough to push Picasso. She gave me my turning point. She showed me who I could be.

I make one more stop before packing it in. I want to see if I can turn on his lights myself, if it will work. When I turn into Adam's street, he is standing in front of his mailbox, and he is smiling. I want to turn back, but it's too late now. I think of his note and the pictures. I should say thank you, but the smile and the hand waving hello are too much. It's too much. Like an idiot, I ride past him, and he steps off the sidewalk into the street, just looking at me. I circle back and aim for the box, but he's laughing now, laughing and holding his hands up, like he's surrendering officially. I ride past him again.

"Is this what you're looking for?" Adam yells as I ride, putting his hand on the mailbox, standing right in front of it. He looks so tall next to that thing. We used to drop new pictures in there when we couldn't wait to share them.

"Do you have anything for me?" he yells.

I don't have any pictures. I just want to touch the mailbox, because that's what I do when I go out. I keep riding around in a circle.

I'm stuck on this invisible rail.

"Wait," he says.

I shake my head and bike faster, around the circle one more time, two more times, while he runs inside. I touch the mailbox and feel relieved, but Adam comes out on his own bike before I can ride away. He takes the outside lane of our invisible track. A dog barks in the neighbor's yard.

We ride around I don't know how many times, around the street he grew up on, around that little island with the massive tree in the middle, the roots spilling toward the edges of the circle. Adam doesn't say a word and I try not to look at him, because I'm embarrassed and this is weird, and it's been a really long day. But I know he's smiling his smile, so I try to relax and listen for the buzz of the spokes as we turn. I want to tell him something, but I don't know where to start, so I just keep riding.

When I speed up, he keeps up; when I slow down, he slows down. He starts laughing first, then I follow him, and we laugh for a couple of rounds, until he says *you are funny* and I say *you have no idea* and he says *I never do* and I look at him, but he's not smiling anymore. He's Adam, focused on something in front of him. Bigger and more than I remembered him. Here is this person, I think. Nice to meet you, I think. Where have you been?

He seems to be reading my mind because, as we approach the next turn, he lets go of the handle and holds out his arm, toward me. There is his huge hand, waiting, and I do grab it, even though I'm scared our bikes will run into each other, even though I've never held Adam's hand.

It's scary when we turn, and we almost lose our balance a bunch of times, but we make it around twice. I don't know who lets go first, but he doesn't follow me down the street, and I don't turn around to look.

When I get home, Mom and Dad are sipping tea and watching *The West Wing* re-runs. Their heads are small and still. That feeling comes over me again, the recognition. That's twice in one day. I take the camera out and aim. My mother turns her head, and I manage to hide the camera before she can smile and say *tomorrow, four o'clock, Ms. K said her door will be open.*

# FIFTEEN

GUESS WHAT I JUST NOTICED.

what?

PABLO.

???

NERUDA AND PICASSO HAVE THE SAME
    FIRST NAME.

they do.

SO DOES MY BROTHER.

right.

TOTAL SIGN.

sign?

THING THAT MEANS SOMETHING.

what does it mean?

NOT CLEAR YET. SOMETHING IMPORTANT.

ok.

HOW IS THE PICTURE?

coming.

YOU SEE? A SIGN.

# SIXTEEN

Before anybody has had their cup of coffee, I'm up and googling Picasso. It's now Tuesday, almost four days after I pushed the sculpture, and I want to remember what it looks like. I sift through pictures and writings about his sculptures until I finally find the one I am looking for. It's a small photograph; it probably belonged in a catalogue. The picture makes the woman look much shorter than I remember her, and it does not really show the texture of the metal, or the shape and light it was reflecting that morning. This picture is lying. It does not look like the thing I pushed. My mom calls my name, and I smell the morning starting.

After saying goodbye and promising to be cooperative during the meeting with Ms. K, I walk to the closest bus stop to ride to Paloma's house and see if I can get some more proof. The brother may not be home, but it's daylight. Maybe I can find something else. Here we go: picture number two. I go over the transportation route in my head, remembering where I have to transfer, and dig through my wallet for my student pass behind the movie cards and coffee receipts. I've had a pass since the eighth grade, when Adam and I were finally allowed to ride Metro on our own.

The N4 bus rolls up. I nod to the driver, show him the card, and move toward the back. Most of the passengers are older, carrying whatever groceries they can, lulled into peace by their daily errands. One woman sings to a baby, in Spanish, about an elephant balancing on a spider-web, bobbing her knees up and down gently. I can't tell if she's trying to keep him awake or put him to sleep. I pull out Paloma's Neruda book. Only one person is talking on her cell phone. The rest are fixed on the city moving past them, or their music, or their shoes. This is what the world looks like when I'm in school. Sleepy and safe. We cross the city and the houses get closer together, more people on the street, coming in and out of stores. I flip to a poem called "We Have Lost Even":

*"Always, always you recede through the evenings / towards where the twilight goes erasing statues."*

I read it in Spanish. *Estatuas.* The word for statues. It's still the middle of the day. No estatuas have been erased yet.

I spot the street and yell *back door* louder than I intended. The lady presses the baby to her chest. It's less than six blocks to Paloma's house and I have to stop to catch my breath, twice. I pass travel agencies, clinics, more bus stops, dollar stores, a rusted playground, restaurants with the smell of chicken and frying corn. The camera trembles in my hands.

In the daylight, the house is neither white nor yellow, something in between. It's sandwiched between two other houses, one bright blue and another bright red. I don't know how I'm supposed to hide. Thank God everybody is at work. Instinctively I look for a room with the lights on, but it's morning. There's nothing to distinguish one room from another. I don't know what I'm looking for. From across the street, where I'm standing, you can't see much. Just a bunch of shadows and reflections. Pablo, the little poet. Or Pablo, the budding Cubist.

Nobody moves inside the house. There are no cars parked in the front. Birds scatter like they can sense the trouble. I stay on this side of the street, put the camera around my neck, and think. Be brave, I tell myself. Stay alert. Let it in. I didn't tell anybody I was coming, so they couldn't be waiting for me. There is no ambush. A small, round woman walks into the front room of the house. She picks something bright from the ground, maybe a toy, and disappears again. A rush of energy fills my head, like the knot at the museum before I pushed the Picasso, and I get the camera ready. *The one who goes for it.* Isn't that what Adam said? Was that yesterday?

I scan the front room and spot a colorful corner where a flame is flickering and beginning to make shadows. It's from a small wooden table against the wall. The table is covered in a pink cloth and there are all kinds of random objects on it. The candle is in the back, made of glass, covered in turquoise paper. In the center, I see a silver frame, with a picture of a woman laughing. The frame is surrounded by orange flowers that look like marigolds. There are two smaller, black-and-white pictures that are yellow around the edges. Those don't have a frame. One is balanced against a coffee tin, and the other is tucked into the strings of a tiny plastic guitar.

I take the picture and count to seventeen in front of the not-quite-yellow house. Then I run to the bus stop. On the slippery bench under a broken shelter, I try my hardest not to break my rule and look at the screen. I'm sure I have found an absolute treasure, that what I saw at Eva's house is some kind of mirage. I want to check if I was dreaming. I can't remember the last time I was this excited about a picture. Was that candy scattered around? Were those Mardi Gras pearls? Was the bowl full of salt or sugar? I want to hear the story that only pictures can tell.

I get on the bus and hide Bogart away under the rest of my things. I move to the back and call Eva right away, clutching my camera bag with the other hand. No texts. I tell her what I saw.

"You found the altar," she says. "What about my brother?"

All that excitement quickly turns into shame, as the bus jerks forward and I grab the sweaty pole to steady myself. She insists she needs a picture of her brother as soon as possible. She sounds more desperate than the last time we spoke.

"I'm sorry, Eva. There was a woman, but I only saw her for a second."

"A woman?" she says. "What did she look like?"

"I don't know. She was kind of short. It was really just a second."

"Young? Old? Light? Dark? What was she doing?"

"I think she was sort of dark…" I whisper, worried about what the other bus riders might think.

Eva huffs, and I start to get annoyed. This was supposed to be my prize picture. I spent months taking pictures of people's front rooms and never found anything as remotely interesting as the altar.

"Well, do you want to see the picture or should I erase it?" I ask.

"Erase it," she says, her voice cold, flat, sharp.

"Fine," I say.

"Erase it and get a picture of my brother."

"I skipped class to get this shot," I say, no longer caring who can hear me.

"You did a lot worse than skip class, Miriam."

"I don't know what you want," I say.

"Yes you do," she says. "I don't need pictures of dead people. It's already been four days. Get me a picture of my brother, or I'll walk over to the Hirshhorn and tell them myself."

I hang up. Everybody on the bus acts like they can't see my eyes welling up. I turn on the camera and look at the picture. It *is* candy, and there are at least four strands of the pearls, some foreign money, a glass of water, and a giant, smooth stone. Whatever story it's telling, Eva can't bear to hear it, but it's too late for me. I want to know.

# SEVENTEEN

"To simplify a radical equation, you have to find the greatest even power."

Mr. L's dry-erase marker squeaks out roots and variables in dark blue. We copy it down in our notebooks, hoping to hang on to the concept long enough to get our homework right. I missed every class except for Calculus today. When it's time to go, I wish I could stay and spend the rest of my day practicing this straightforward task, in this room, with my quiet, patient, odorless teacher. But after everyone's left, Mr. L just gathers his things and asks me if I'll do him the favor of turning out the lights when I go.

So I go.

"Have a seat, Miriam. You're a little early," Ms. K says when I knock on her office door.

"Yes, sorry."

"No problem, but I'd rather have your parents here before we start."

"Okay," I say.

"It's a family meeting, and you—*we*—might say something they should hear as well."

"Right. That makes sense."

Ms. K sips her tea and checks her email. I bet she has a Facebook page. I bet she's bummed about the schoolwide lock. I bet she's friends with Jon Stewart. The sound of the keyboard is driving me crazy.

"So, do you like it here?" I ask.

She turns her head toward me, but her fingers are still typing. She's wearing a headband, and I swear she's got the smallest ears I've ever seen. They're not pointy, like elves'; just baby ears, like they didn't grow with the rest of her.

"Yes," she says. "It's a great school."

I fatten my lips and nod.

"Do you like your job?" I ask.

Ms. K moves to one of the armchairs facing my couch. She tucks her long skirt between her legs before crossing them. She doesn't seem annoyed that I interrupted her work. Maybe no one has asked her whether she likes it yet. The rings on her fingers are made of either plastic or glass. Tapping them seems inappropriate, but I want to. God knows why I want to.

"I love my job," she says, looking straight at me.

"That's good," I tell her. "You're lucky."

That's what my father is always saying. *Find a job you*

*love, Miriam. Do what you love, Miriam. Make sure you care, Miriam. Follow your passion, Miriam.*

"I know I'm lucky," Ms. K answers, smiling. "And so are you."

I almost laugh.

"Do you feel lucky?" she asks.

"Should we be talking about this?" I ask. "Before my parents get here?"

"I asked the question," she says.

"Lucky how?" I ask. "I mean—I know I'm lucky. I go to a school with a big lawn and Ivy League teachers and photo labs. I've got a darkroom in my basement, a house with a porch. There are people who don't have anything. Of course I am *lucky.*"

"I'm not really talking about school, or your house."

My face is hot. "What are you talking about?"

She uncrosses her legs and leans her elbows on her knees, getting closer.

"Well, you have parents who care about you, good friends…"

"Yes, sure…"

Ms. K is mad focused now. She just switched it on, like a social work ninja. She looks like she's waiting for something.

"…but does that mean I'm lucky?"

"What do you think?" she says.

I think I'm a dragonfly in your spiderweb, that's what I think. That's not what I say.

"I don't know. You're right. I have people, but you found what you love, you know? You can give me random assignments and help people get it together. You enjoy it. You must feel powerful and important and like you did something at the end of the day. Don't you?"

"What do *you* love, Miriam?" she says in this soft, eerie voice. I know it's an open question, but I still feel like I'm supposed to get it right.

"What do I *love*?" I say.

"Yes."

"Like—what do I love *doing* or what do I love, like, in the *world*?"

She doesn't clarify. She just waits again, like a comatose crocodile ready to pounce. Eva would have so much to say here. This would be a dangerous question for Eva. This is exactly what I should ask her the next time we meet.

Adam loves viewfinders, and donuts, and the horrible orange and brown color scheme in the Metro. He also loves mornings, and anything west of Minnesota, and, for a while, those super-salty cod strips you can get at the Japanese store in the burbs. He loves Guns N' Roses and Jay Z and that sorry gazebo they built to commemorate the World War I soldiers. He would pay you to shampoo his hair for half an hour straight, and he was pissed when they took the panda back to China.

"I don't know, Ms. K. I have to think about that."

Elliot loves music, and biographies of musicians, and obscure music venues where the bouncers are vegan. He loves the ocean, and Old Bay fries, and gangster movies that are not *The Godfather*. He loves birds and leather, and he especially loves my behind. He loved every picture I took, and he loved how warm my hands were, and Arlington in the snow.

I don't know what I love.

The clock above Ms. K's head says four, and, like yodeling Austrians in a cuckoo clock, my parents pop through the office door.

My mother walks in first, her thousands bracelets rattling as she shakes Ms. K's hands. My father gives her his best flash-fiction smile and puts his hand on my shoulder, squeezing it hello. I find this mix of determination and anxiety unbearable.

"Take a seat," Ms. K offers, and they settle next to me on the sofa. Dad's thin navy socks are sagging under his work suit. He is by far the most uncomfortable person in the room.

My father has always explained every little thing to me. He's always had full confidence in my ability to reason. From taking turns at the slide to ordering my own breakfast at the diner, he's never missed an opportunity to teach me something: how to be kind, how to play fair, how to persist.

*You got that, Miriam?* he always said. If I looked vacant or tired as I nodded, he would ask me to repeat what I learned until he felt sure he had given me something to hold on to. *Good. Now, put that in your life pocket, Miriam.*

Today he looks like he's coming to collect.

"So, I'm sure you've all been to parent-teacher conferences before, but is this is the first time you've met with a social worker?"

My parents nod. Mom hasn't looked at me since she walked in the door.

"So, we're here to talk about Miriam, and to address some of the issues that have come up in the past week."

Mom is nodding so hard her head might snap off, and every time she nods, the bracelets jingle like back-up singers.

"Miriam is a talented artist, a smart young woman, and a good student. Everybody knows you are an exceptional photographer."

That makes four times she's called me talented since we met. I look at Mom, the real photographer, but her eyes are unwavering. She is completely committed to Ms. K. Dad cracks a quick smile, crosses his legs, and pulls at the hem of his pants.

Ms. K tells them about what the teachers said, about how nobody is here to judge and they all just want to help.

Dad breaks in.

"I'm sorry to interrupt," he says. "Miriam"—he's looking at me now—"do you know what Ms. Kiper is talking about? Do you know why we're worried?"

"Because I'm more quiet than I used to be?"

"That too. You also took everything off your walls and painted your room a sad green color. And you mess with your mom's dinners. But let's start with an easy one. Why were you late to the bus on Friday?"

"I was not feeling well. And I went to the Winogrand."

"Which one, Miriam?" he asks.

"Both."

"That's not true."

Mom's voice comes from the end of the couch, and

she refuses to look at me. Shit. I forgot about her talk with Adam. He must've told her.

Ms. K looks confused. "Weren't you sick?" she asks.

"I was," I say. "I was sick and I was going to the Winogrand. I was on my way and that's when I got sick, so I didn't go. I didn't get there."

Mom frowns. Ms. K pushes her knuckles against her lips. She's thinking.

"I'm sorry," she says to my parents. "Is there something I should know?"

"Well," Mom says, "I don't know if it matters."

"What is it, Sarah?" Dad says.

What is it, Sarah? I think. Out with it, Sarah.

"She described the Winogrand pictures."

Dad throws his hands up. "I don't get it. Go on."

"She means that Miriam wanted her to believe she was at the exhibit," Ms. K says, slowly re-animating.

"It means she lied," Mom says.

"All right, let's not get too carried away over this," Dad interjects. "Miriam, why did you tell Mom you were there?"

I scan Ms. K's expression, which has gone from condescension to mild panic, like she may have left the gas on at home. She looks like something's struck her, but she's not sure what.

"I didn't want her to worry," I answer.

"Well, obviously … "

"Is this what this meeting is about?" I interrupt, exasperated by their interrogation tactics.

Dad smooths back his graying hair, what's left of the

thick head of curls I used to pull at when I rode on his shoulders. *Ouch, bean, don't pull so hard. But I'm going to fall. No you won't, I'm holding your ankles. But you're so tall. Don't worry bean, you're not going to fall.*

"Miriam," he says, his tone more gentle now, "what's going on?"

"Nothing's going on, Dad. I've just been a little off."

Ms. K sighs. The panic is gone from her face now. The only thing left is defeat.

"Miriam, I'd like to give you a chance to tell your parents yourself."

This is it. Here it comes. My father covers his nose and mouth with his hands like he is praying, then he looks at my mother, who has lost all motion, and back at me. This room is a still. The whole world is nothing but landscape.

"Tell us what, Miriam?" he says, raising his voice a little. I wait.

"Miriam skipped her afternoon classes yesterday, and she hasn't been in school all morning today," Ms. K says, serious as a stroke.

"*What?*" My father looks at my mother for an explanation, but even her bracelets have lost their voice. "She skipped classes to go where?"

Ms. K points to my corner with her eyebrows. My father is exasperated, but all I feel is relief. It was not the sculpture. I skipped class. This was her big news.

"Okay, Miriam, where were you?" he says, losing his patience.

Taking an unappreciated picture of an altar in Columbia Heights.

"I was not feeling well. I went home."

Dad rolls his eyes. "Sarah?"

My mother shakes her head.

"Did you know this?" he asks her.

"No."

"Well, was she home when you got there yesterday?"

"Yes, Seth. She's seventeen. She wakes up. She takes a shower. She goes to school. She comes home. She goes off. She comes back."

"If I can say something…" Ms. K interjects. Here we go. Ms. K pulls out a clipboard with a piece of paper and a pen.

"Miriam, is it okay if I ask you a few questions, in front of your parents?"

Dad wiggles his nose to adjust his glasses, which breaks my heart. I try not to look at either one of them.

"Sure," I say.

"How have you been sleeping?" she asks.

I stop for a minute. I can't tell if this is a trick question. Maybe Adam told her about the pictures. Maybe my parents know I've been sneaking out. They don't look guilty, though, or even angry. They just look confused.

"Okay," I lie.

She checks a box on her sheet.

"Have you been eating?"

I think back to this morning's muffin, still wrapped on the bottom of my bag.

"I've been feeling a little sick, so not as much as usual."

She checks another box.

"Do you feel tired all the time?"

"Not all the time. But yes, a little. I mean, a lot. Sometimes."

"Do you think she's depressed?" Dad asks.

"Not necessarily."

I'm sure this is the kind of vague language that makes Dad want to reach across the room and choke the social worker.

"Our time is almost up," Ms. K says, "but I've given Miriam an assignment."

"Good," Dad says. "What kind of assignment?"

"It's a project."

"Like an apology, or a reflection…?" He's trying to remember the kind of punishment teachers used to give when he got in trouble, to make you think, to give you a little shame.

"Miriam, why don't you tell your parents?"

"I have to give her five pictures."

I detect a stirring in my mother's corner. I don't think Dad remembers anything like this from his school days.

"Yes," Ms. K says with a hint of pride, "five new pictures."

The couch is trembling a little, and my mother's bracelets slide down her arm all at once as she brings her hand to her mouth in a familiar gesture. She's laughing. When she starts like this, she cannot stop. Dad is exasperated, but Mom has gone completely bananas. Ms. K uncrosses her legs again, and rests my file on her lap, waiting and smiling nervously.

"I'm sorry," Mom says between fits of loud giggles, fanning her hands in front of her face.

I haven't seen her laugh like this since we missed the plane to my Opa's funeral. She has a tendency to laugh through disasters. Dad strokes his neck, where a strange rash seems to have sprouted.

"I can't stop," she says with tears in her eyes. "Sorry, I'm just tired. I didn't get much sleep last night."

Good thing I didn't go out last night. Since I took the first picture for Eva, I've been sleeping through the night like a baby who no longer needs her mother. Dad rubs his palms all over his face and then glares at Mom, who shrugs and surrenders.

"It's okay," Ms. K offers, slightly cold. "There's a lot of tension in this room. Laughter is a way to—"

"Are the pictures a kind of therapy or something?" Dad interrupts.

Mom, who had managed to be quiet for a minute, now loses it again.

Dad gives her a look and forges on. "Sarah, I'm trying to figure out what the pictures might do for Miriam. You said any pictures she wants, right?"

Mom excuses herself to go the bathroom, and I swear I hear her mumbling "pictures, pictures" on her way out the door. Poor Ms. K. I feel sorry for her and her tiny ears.

"I'm sorry, I don't understand," Dad continues. "I'm not an expert, but you're telling me Miriam has skipped school, and she can't tell us why, and we're not sure why we're here, but what we are going to do about it is *take some pictures*? You know she started taking pictures when she was three years old, right? It's second nature for Miriam. It's nothing. It's easy."

"That's what *I'm* going to do about it," Ms. K says, cool as a fucking cucumber, making her comeback. "Would you like to talk about what *you're* going to do?"

Dad relaxes in a manner that suggests not defeat but interest. His toes squeak inside the tight leather of his good shoes. Amazingly, he has no comments to make.

"Have you taken any pictures yet?" Ms. K asks, looking at me.

Dad turns toward me. I'm caught off guard.

"Yes. I have."

"Good, I guess. Good," he says.

"Do you have anything you want to say, Miriam?" Ms. K asks.

"I'm sorry?" I say.

"I think your parents want to make sure you'll be honest with them, and that you'll come to school, so we can all help you through this."

"Two pictures," I say. "I already took two."

"Good," Ms. K says.

Dad sighs, just loud enough to let me know he's on to me, that he doesn't fully buy it.

"I'm taking you to school in the morning, Miriam."

"Dad, you don't have to ... "

"I am. For a little while. And I'd like for you to meet with Ms. Kiper again."

Ms. K nods in approval. The mother may be nuts, but at least the father is cooperating. I nod.

"We'll all meet again, after she hands in her pictures," Ms. K tries to reassures us. Dad looks at the door, hoping Mom will walk in with an apologetic apple crumble. No sign.

"Sure. Thank you for your time and your help. Sarah and I will be in touch."

They shake hands. I smile at Ms. K. We walk out to find Mom cornered by Mr. Green, the Photo teacher. In a moment of great tenderness and (let's face it) pity, my father stuffs the car keys in the pocket of my jacket and nudges me toward the exit. I'm so relieved to escape, I run down the hall on my tiptoes so they won't notice me. I'm glad Mom is there to distract him. The Green has always had a bit of a photo crush on her.

# EIGHTEEN

what do u love?

# NINETEEN

The car smells like wet paper cups. I switch the radio on. It's playing a sleepy song Elliot might have liked. The voice is high but not whiny, and there's a super synthesized choir that makes it all sound like it's lifting, a little like that night at the show. I watch my parents walk back to the car. Mom motions for Dad to drive.

"I have to go back to work for a while. Do you want to get some food before we go home?" he says.

"I can make pasta ... " she says.

"I thought maybe it would be easier to get some food."

"Whatever you want."

No word on Mr. Green or the giggling fit in Ms. K's room. No word on the skipping.

"What do you want to eat, Miriam?" Mom asks.

"Whatever."

She sighs.

"Look, I shouldn't have laughed like that, right in front of your teacher."

"Not my teacher ... "

"Fine. Your counselor, Ms. K. I don't know what happened. It was so tense in there, and you weren't talking, and Dad was sweating like crazy, and when she told us about the assignment, it all seemed so ... "

"Ridiculous?" I offer.

"Absurd."

My chest tightens at how appropriate the word is, for everything from the sculpture to Eva's photo request to the meetings with Ms. K. We just spent half an hour with a woman who is *trained* to rescue people with real problems, and all we did was fidget about missing class. Then we scheduled another meeting.

At the next intersection, a crossing guard stops us with her palm and keeps her hand there while she greets the kids and parents by their names, telling them she'll see them tomorrow, inquiring after their collapsing art projects, praising their choice of glittery shoes. The spires of the Cathedral show themselves behind the hilltop. I remember the organ.

"Actually," I say, with unexpected purpose, "could you drop me off at the library on Wisconsin? I want to check out some books for another project."

My parents look at each other for consensus, which I have always found comforting. Mom's hair spills through the headrest as she looks over to give me the green light.

"Be home for dinner, all right?" she says.

"No more lies, Miriam," Dad adds. "No more skip-ping class."

I nod. "Thank you, guys. Thanks for coming today."

They beam at my nugget of appreciation, and I feel dirty but relieved. *Sure, bean. No problem, love. Any time. Of course. We're here for you. We'll get through this. This is good, it's all right. No big deal.* And on and on until a delivery truck honks at us and I'm pushing the heavy doors into the land of carpet and germs and ideas protected by shiny, plastic coats.

REAL MEN READ, a poster behind the library desk announces. Except it's all women peering at me from behind their glasses, taking a pause from inputting the lat-est bar code, casting a side-glance from behind their carts. I remember that librarians don't speak unless spoken to.

"Excuse me," I say, "where's the art section?"

"Past the computers, in the back left corner."

I smile and head to the art section, where I drop my bag next to a dusty armchair.

I go for the photo books first and end up with a pile of Adam's favorites—Robert Frank, Lee Friedlander, good old HCB. I like their portraits best. They're almost perfect. You can see the fear in people's eyes, and the thrill. Every-body likes to be looked at, but most people don't really like to be seen. These guys can really show you a person.

I think of Eva's face and try hard to keep the image. It's hard to remember a face, even when you sit down and concentrate. You can remember a scar, or a mole. But the rest is just outlines, or a certain look they gave you. Like Elliot, for example. I see him around sometimes, but I'm losing his face in my memory. I can remember the sculpture better than I can remember his face up close.

I wonder if I've really lost him, if he was something I let go of while swimming in the ocean the day of the fight, and now I can never get him back, because the ocean is way too big and I would not know where to start. I think of Eva and how sure she sounded when she said things never stay the same. How could that be Elliot I saw on the carousel—when I'm not even allowed to go in there, stop the horses, yank him off and away from another girl? He is not mine, but does that mean he's gone? Can someone be right in front of you and just be gone?

I put the books back on the shelf and work my way down the alphabet, tracing the spines with my fingers. There are at least ten books about Picasso—the sculptures, the paintings, the biographies. I pick a book of portraits. If only I could take pictures that looked like this. Half profile, half frontal, orange and purple faces, faces with one eye open and the other shut. Photography is so limited, so rigid. Painters are the real face-makers. I would never forget a face that looked like this.

I want to study the book a little longer, but they're going to close soon. At the desk, the lady tells me I need proof of residency to get a library card, and I nearly break into a sob. I just want to take the book home.

I show her my bus card, my pool card, my school ID, my expired driver's permit. I recite my address and phone number at impressive speeds. When she starts to bite her lip and lower her eyes, I name every stop on the red Metro line from Bethesda to Silver Spring.

"My mom used to take me to the organ rehearsals at the Cathedral, down the street."

She smiles, probably at my stubbornness, and, with the look of a girl who's been flirted with, she hands me a card.

"Enjoy your book," she says.

This sweater weather cleans everything up, and I'm almost convinced I can handle whatever is coming, that I'm strong enough. I take out my camera, but instead of taking a picture, I look at the altar photo again. I'm not erasing it. Eva doesn't have to know. The book is heavy and awkward in my tote, but the day is almost done. The meeting with Ms. K is over. At least I have one less lie to keep track of.

Walking home, I stop at a light next to a woman with a giant belly. Only one of her coat buttons is fastened, and she is patting her bump gently. We walk across the street together, and I hang back so it won't be awkward. She's going the same way I'm going. She's probably coming home from work, and I imagine her husband kissing her on the cheek, bringing her a glass of water, maybe drawing circles around their future baby.

As she turns the corner, presumably onto her street, I remember my period hasn't come, but I have no husband. Elliot will not teach this baby about good music. Elliot will not fall asleep with this baby on his chest.

My hands reach for my belly before I can stop them, feeling for a bump. There's nothing but the usual, reasonable bit of chub. It's still soft. Nobody would guess anything was preparing to grow in there. The more I indulge, the more I realize that I've crossed a line—or better, a wall—in my mind, and it becomes a little more impossible to return to denial.

I wish my most persistent thoughts could be like the foamy fat floating in one of Mom's long-simmering soups, that I could skim them off with a shallow wooden spoon and enjoy my dinner like nothing gross was ever there, only what's good for me. When I get home, I brush my shoes on the welcome mat before going inside, even if they're clean, even if I know I'll take them off as soon as I walk in. When the door shuts behind me, she's there, in her jeans, my Sarah, my mother. Her hands are orange and sticky.

"I'm carving," she says.

"For Halloween," I say.

"Yup," she says, and her face softens into a question I can't answer yet.

I sit next to her in the kitchen and watch her make the eyes first, then the crooked teeth and finally scraping it all clean. When she's done, she sets it on our bench, on top of an old magazine.

At dinner, we make fun of her outburst in Ms. K's office, and Dad asks if he can see the two pictures I was talking about. Mom smirks and explains my rules to him, and he looks as if he understands. After washing the dishes, my mom lays out the newspaper and takes out the knife. It's the first time in months I feel like the daughter they might have been missing.

Dad gives me a kiss on top of my head before going to bed and asks if I want to read *Captains Courageous*, the book he used to read to me as a kid. I can't tell if it's a joke, but he waves me off playfully before I get the chance to ask, a nostalgic look in his eyes. I tell him he'll have to find it first, and he says maybe he will.

Upstairs, in my bed, I try to remember what the walls used to look like before I took everything down. Nothing ever stays the same. The book of Neruda poems is on the floor where I left it. I read the last one: "The Song of Despair."

*"You swallowed everything, like distance. / Like the sea, like time."*

I open the window and the air rushes in to bite me.

# TWENTY

PABLO.

# TWENTY-ONE

I wake up from the smell at first. Then I feel the warmth between my legs, and that's when I see the stain on my bed. I stumble to the bathroom, take everything off, and throw my underwear in the trash. The blood is dark red, darker than I remembered it. I look through the cabinets for a tampon and don't even bother to use soap when I rinse my hands. There it is, I think in the mirror. No baby.

I thought what I would feel was huge, unmistakable relief. It's different though. I'm embarrassed to say it feels lonely, and hard. No baby. No husband. No heroic purpose in life. It's just me, the way I wasn't before. On the way back up from the dryer, with a new pair of underwear and sweats on, I see the pumpkin is now on our porch.

I find a fresh tea light in the junk drawer and light it with the Shabbat matches. I open the door slowly, so I won't wake anybody up. I usually leave from the garage for my night prowls, and opening the front door seems more dangerous. I say a silent blessing in my head for the dirty underwear, for myself, for my Mom who is upstairs worrying about things she can't imagine. I lift the pumpkin lid and place the flame in there. It's cold on the porch, in the dark, four days before Halloween. I peer through the jack-o'-lantern's eyes to watch the orange shadows. It's spooky and soothing at the same time. I remember the way this felt when I was a kid, like some kind of magic was being released, the kind that would scare children on any other day.

Halloween was incredible. It meant I could hold my dad's hand in the dark and let it go at every house, running toward the candy as they watched and waited for me to come back. I could be an insect, a planet, a warty witch. It meant we could play with death a little, take charge of our greatest fears as we walked around with fake guts and fake blood and fake teeth and fake swords. We could be bad guys without feeling guilty or scared. All kinds of exiled creatures could come out and play. My own mommy could carve mean eyes with a butcher knife and all the kids would squeal in delight.

Before getting back into bed, I check my phone and see Eva's response again.

PABLO.

That's what she loves. Not poetry, not music, not even her mother. Pablo. She sounded desperate on the phone this morning. I start to think up all kinds of horrors. Why does she want to see the boy so badly? What's making her so afraid? Why wouldn't she just stay with him? I consider calling the police, but that would be impossible. I don't even know her last name, and I couldn't really explain why or how I know her aunt's address. Anyway, the police don't come because you're imagining things, and if Eva's family hasn't found her yet, they must trust her, or not care. Maybe they kicked her out themselves.

I imagine what Pablo might look like, whether his hair is black like Eva's, if he speaks Spanish or English or both, like the poems Neruda wrote. I think of that last poem I read:

*"Oh the mad coupling of hope and force / in which we merged and despaired."*

Hope and force, hope and fear, hope and loss—hope being the superhero, the tea light in the orange pumpkin. With hope and force, I take twenty dollars out of our money box and call for a cab to come pick me up a block from here. On the way out, I pick up the jack-o'-lantern. The cab driver is listening to the radio in a foreign language, oblivious to my age, my pajamas, my pumpkin cargo. We ride across the city and it only takes ten minutes to get to Eva's house.

He waits inside the car as I step out quickly and put the jack-o'-lantern on top of their porch steps, the tea light still inside. Maybe one day I'll have a kid who will look through the carved eyes, but not now, and it won't be Elliot's. This one's for Pablo. Here it is, little guy: the world is a scary wonder.

In the car, the driver is arguing on the phone, so he doesn't mind when I ask if he can wait a second before going back home and whether it would be all right to roll down my window. He just nods. It's cold. I pull out Bogart, aim from inside the car, and take a picture of my pumpkin on Pablo's steps.

# TWENTY~TWO

r u awake?

YUP.

getting colder?

YUP.

where r u?

YOU?

on my way home. got a picture.

SUPER. IT'S LATE.

i know. i read the song of despair.

GOOD ONE.

how do you say that in spanish?

WHAT?

despair.

DESESPERANZA.

and hope?

ESPERANZA.

aha. despair = without hope.

YOU GOT IT.

not me. you?

NEVER.

# TWENTY-THREE

My breath sputters in the morning chill. I'm waiting for my dad to bring the car around, because he takes pride in being a gentleman. My mom is still inside looking for the house keys. I am standing right where the pumpkin was yesterday, hoping she won't notice, trying to keep it cool. Mom bursts through the door with her wool coat unbuttoned. Dad honks and she sticks out her tongue.

"Hi," I say.

"Hey. Let's go," she says. "We're all late."

We hurry into the car, and, after a little back and forth, they decide it's best to drop me off first. We ride through Rock Creek, on the parkway, where the leaves are on fire and the joggers are already wearing hats. This is really my favorite time of year. I eat my re-heated bagel to make Mom happy. It's so chewy that my jaw keeps clicking. I can tell Dad's doing his best not to turn the radio on, that he wants to give us room to talk.

"It's so pretty," my mom says. "We should all go for a hike this weekend."

"Sure," Dad says. "What do you think, bean?"

"A hike would be nice," I say.

"Hey bean, you want me to pick you up today?" he says, taking his eyes off the road to look back at me in the mirror.

"No thanks, Dad. I can take the bus."

"You sure? I could sneak out of work early for a day."

"Don't worry, Dad. I'll take the bus."

"With Adam?" he asks.

"No," I say, "by myself."

The rest of the ride, we sit in silence, and he turns around to pat my knee when it's time to go in.

"Go get 'em, bean. I'll see you tonight."

Mom blows me a kiss.

"Thanks for the ride," I tell them, resolving to go buy another pumpkin and carve an identical face.

"My pleasure," he says, and they wait until I'm out of sight to leave and finally turn on the morning news.

It's early, so I grab a cup of coffee in the cafeteria, which I haven't done since last year, pre-Elliot. "Hey Miriam!" says Stella. "Yo, Miriam," barks Jason. Victor nods. Elle waves. Rachel walks backwards and reminds me of a Students For Sudan meeting she thinks I would "dig." The faces thrown aside by my relationship with Elliot are coming back like happy, unoffended ghosts. No one seems to mind that I went under water for a year. They moved on. Elliot's with Maggie now. For all intents and purposes, I'm back.

I have five minutes.

While I change my tampon, some girls walk into the bathroom blaring a techno song. Their voices sound vaguely familiar, but I can't tell with the song so loud.

"Oh my God, I love this one," one of them squeaks.

"It's a remix of an old song by this jazz singer. It's AMAZ-ING."

I hide in the stall, hoping I can finish my business before we get to the amazing part. Oh man. It's Nina Simone. They went and remixed Nina Simone. It makes me incredibly sad, so sad I just sit there, waiting for it to end. Maybe they will play something decent next, something that doesn't feel like your soul is getting whipped by a synthetic snare drum.

Halfway through, I give up and open the door. Maggie and two other girls are standing by the sink. Something in my chest collapses, like a butterfly chair. And all of my breath goes to that space, runs through it and gets sucked in before it can ever get to the other side. The girls look away immediately, but Maggie smiles a little, the thick pink soap in her hand.

We all wash our hands while the excruciating song wraps up. I let them walk out first, and give them a few minutes to get a head start. Elliot—the guy who brought me to see music I could hardly stand it was so good, the one who lugs a massive string instrument into this building every Wednesday. Elliot—the boy who lies on his carpet and holds my hand through three albums in Icelandic. That

Elliot has fallen in love with a girl who thinks nothing of murdering a beautiful song, a girl who isn't too snobby or proud to say hello to me, a girl who most definitely doesn't steal her mother's jack-o'-lantern. Elliot has fallen in love with a nice, lighthearted girl who will not drown him in a painful, metaphorical ocean.

Everything in my body is a little off balance. My right arm is longer than my left, my hip is sharp against my jeans, my face is cold on one side and hot on the other. All the organs and limbs are answering to some random role call in no particular order. *I'm here*, the spleen says; *don't forget me*, the heel cries; *keep me safe*, the mind orders. I shush them as soon as they make themselves known, but there is no way out of this. This body is mine. I can't crawl out of it and leave it limp on the linoleum. I'm going to have to carry it down the hall, into the chair, behind the table, and all the way through everything I do from now on.

I. Am. Still. Here.

# TWENTY-FOUR

Comparative Literature, Modern European History, Free, Lunch, Theory of Knowledge, Calculus. I promised I would not skip class. During my free period, I take my laptop outside to the Cave. The Cave is the place people go when they want to be left alone. It's the campus blind spot. Every high school has one.

Adam and I came here to take secret portraits, our first experiment in guerrilla photography. I wanted to be a documentarian, like Dorothea. Adam wanted to find the Americans, like Robert Frank. He said this is where people hide, and the only thing people hide is the truth, and man did we love the truth. Back then I was always looking for people and their insides. I wanted to find their dreams and name their pain, like the portraits in yesterday's books. Now I wait until everyone's asleep and snap up the leftovers, like a vulture.

We called our subjects "pilgrims," and justified our breach of ethics by telling ourselves we were documenting our times: anxious, hopeful, lonely. We came out here three of four times a week for almost a year. It's basically what we did with the second half of freshman year.

Some days we would get nothing, and other days we'd walk back with real treasures, too giddy or guilty to even boast. Hunter, the badass, reading *Harry Potter* and smoking Lucky Strikes. Justin cheating on Sammy with the smartest girl in our grade. Kalima rolling out a prayer mat on a bed of rotting leaves. Carla making small cuts above her ankle with a bright pink Bic blade.

Miriam, art vandal and pumpkin thief, I sit on our rock, open up my laptop, and start typing. I am officially a pilgrim.

*Dear Mom and Dad,*

*First of all, I would like to say sorry for everything I've put you through. After all, you did push me on the swing, and you gave me my first camera, and you paid for me to go to a school where the counselor gives you tea and knows when you skipped one class. I know I've been a bit of a shmuck lately and here is why.*

Try again.

*Dear Mom and Dad,*

*Remember this summer when I came home early from Elliot's house? And I called you from the station*

*and you asked me what happened and when I said*
*nothing you just asked me what I needed? That was*
*really great. I really appreciate that. I was so scared*
*and it smelled pretty bad on the train and my bathing*
*suit was still wet from the ocean and all I wanted to*
*do was get home. You guys looked so tired when you*
*picked me up. And then we got some Lebanese food*
*and we ate and you asked me a million unrelated*
*questions and I just told you we broke up and Mom*
*asked why and Dad, you said, we don't have to know*
*why, it doesn't matter why, and I was so jealous of you*
*because you are a man.*

Not quite.

*Mom and Dad,*

*I'm trying to tell you the truth about everything*
*because I literally don't think my body can take*
*it anymore, but I don't know where to start. You*
*know the Picasso sculpture at the Hirshhorn? Well, I*
*knocked it down. That's why I was late to the bus. I*
*don't think it broke. Anyway, this girl saw me do it*
*and I went to meet her because I was lonely, I think,*
*and scared and so so angry. It's nothing you guys did.*
*Really. I was just feeling like you were looking for me*
*all the time, and not finding me, like I was hiding*
*in some closet and you wanted to yank me out. But*
*I was there the whole time, Mom. I am still your*
*Miriam. Do you see that?*

Shit.

*Dear Mom and Dad,*

*After the summer, Elliot came to say he was sorry. We slept together for the last time, and then he left me. I thought I was pregnant. Then I pushed the Picasso and met a girl who is in trouble, and I don't know how to help her, but I want to. I also stole your pumpkin for her little brother. I'm not pregnant.*

God fucking damn it.

*Dear Mom and Dad,*

*I pushed the sculpture, and I don't know what to do. I don't want everything to change, but either way it does. I think it already has. I miss you. I love you. Don't tell Adam.*

I save all the letters in a folder I call TRY AGAIN and then drop that folder between old essays, internship cover letters, and term papers. I missed lunch, but I have a bag of pretzels in my bag, so I eat them on my way back to Theory of Knowledge, where we explore the "big questions" of philosophers who tend to die tragically. Socrates was sentenced and drank himself to death; Descartes caught a really bad cold; Spinoza inhaled glass dust; Foucault died of AIDS. I have to make it through the day. Let's see what the ancients can do for me.

# TWENTY~FIVE

I NEED YOU.

where r u?

DO YOU HAVE THE PICTURE?

yes.

CAN YOU MEET ME IN GEORGETOWN?

r u ok?

JUST COME.

can u meet me at school?

FINE. GIVE ME TWENTY MINUTES.

# TWENTY~SIX

First thing I see is my green sweater walking fast up the hill. I walk out to meet her, so we can start getting farther away from whoever might be watching. Eva looks terrible. She looks like she's slept about two hours in the last two days. Her skin is more ash than brown, and her hair is greasy and pasted to the top of her head.

"Are you okay?" I ask.

"I'm fine," she says, smiling a little. "Hey, I'm sorry about what I said on the phone the other day. About going to the museum and telling on you. I was really worked up."

"I get it," I say. "It's been a rough couple of days for me too."

"Is the guy bothering you again?"

I smirk. "No. Actually, the guy is pretty much lost, I think."

"Oh. Well, sometimes that's better," she says, her hands in her pocket.

"Yeah," I say. "Anyway, I have the picture. You want to sit somewhere?"

"No, that's okay. Can I just see it?"

"All right, but you have to promise not to get pissed. It's not in the daylight, but it's proof that he's there, like you asked."

"I promise," she says, and puts her hand on her heart. It's shaking.

I hand Bogart over and show her the picture of the pumpkin, bracing for the worst.

It takes her a while to figure it out, then she smiles a really tender smile, a small upward crack in the tired plaster her face has become, and I think that maybe lying and stealing are not so bad, if it can make someone so tired smile.

She gives me the camera back and doesn't say a word. Instead, she just sits down, right there on someone's sloping lawn. I stay standing. The silence is really scaring me.

"We've never done that," she says.

"What do you mean?" I ask.

"We never carved a pumpkin together," she says.

Fuck, fuck, fucking fuck.

"I'm glad they did that with him. He must have loved it."

"Can I ask you something?" I say.

She doesn't answer.

"Do you have a place to sleep?" I ask.

She laughs. "Is it because I look like shit?"

"Well …"

"I really do," she says. "You want to see something?"

She untangles her hair from the rubber band and runs her hands through it. It stands out like a greasy lion's mane.

"It's bad, huh?" She smiles again.

"It's pretty bad," I say.

She smells her armpits. "I smell too, right?"

I shrug.

"No, seriously, smell me."

"No thanks."

"Come on. Come and smell me and tell me I don't smell like a fucking pigeon."

And that does it. I start laughing like I haven't laughed in years, tears-in-my-eyes, peeing-in-my-pants laughing. Every time I look up, she's holding up her greasy hair and motioning for me to come closer, and it makes me laugh even harder, until I can barely breathe.

When it's over, I feel completely empty.

Eva straightens up and braids her dirty hair.

"Let me see the altar photo," she says.

"Now you want to see the altar?" I joke.

"Don't make me beg," she says.

I scroll to the picture, and Eva sighs and squints and sighs again.

"How did you know I didn't erase it?"

"Magic," she says.

"Of course. I do love that picture," I say.

She pulls the gold fish out from underneath her sweater and holds on to it.

"Hey, Eva, seriously, do you have a place to sleep?"

She turns to face me. "Don't worry about me. I'll make you a deal. If you get me one more picture, I'll wash my hair."

"I'm serious," I say.

"So am I. Dead serious."

"I really think . . . "

"What?" she says—sharp, loud.

"I really think you should go back home," I say.

"I told you I can't right now," she says.

"I know you said your mom was sick, but don't you think it's better if you go through it together?"

"My mom doesn't need me anymore," she says.

"Maybe not, but Pablo does," I say.

She says something in Spanish.

"I don't understand," I say.

"No," she says, "you don't. Here. Here's a key to the house. I'm sending you there. Do whatever you need. Tell them. Don't tell them. Just get me a picture of Pablo. Meet me at the zoo tomorrow, at four, in front of the cheetahs, and I swear to God I'll leave you alone."

She puts the key in my bag and walks away. I swear to my God, leaving is the last thing I want her to do.

# TWENTY~SEVEN

**Mom:** You won't believe what happened.

**Me:** What?

**Mom:** Somebody took our jack-o'-lantern.

**Me:** Oh. Really?

**Mom:** Yeah. Who does that?

**Me:** I don't know. Maybe some kids
thought it might be funny.

**Mom:** It's not funny.

**Me:** I'm sorry.

**Mom:** It's okay. I got another one.

**Me:** Really?

**Mom:** Of course. You want to help me carve?

**Me:** Sure. Can we make it different?

**Mom:** Okay. What do you want?
  Bat? Ghost? Scary face?

**Me:** Ghost.

**Mom:** Ghost it is.

# TWENTY~EIGHT

"Excuse me Mama. Mama? Do you know that if that cheetah wanted to, it could eat you in five seconds and jump
over the fence and grab you and you cannot stop it because
it's the fastest animal in the world, faster than your car and
an airplane and even faster than a whale and the whole
ocean when there are big, enormous waves?"

"Wow, really?" Her voice is engaged, but she's looking
at a map of the zoo.

"Yes. Really. AND it can jump with all the legs at the
same time like this, but it has four legs, and also it has spots.
But it doesn't climb trees like the leopard so don't worry. It
won't fall on your head."

"Good," the mama says.

"Yeah. Good. But if you look at the tiger in her eyes,
she'll get scared, because she doesn't want to see your eyes,
because she's walking near the water, and she's hungry."

"You want to go see the tiger?" Mama asks.

"Okay. But don't look at her," he answers.

"I won't."

"I will look at her, but not in her eyes."

"Sounds good," Mama says.

"Yeah," he answers.

"Let's go."

The mother and child disappear into the mini-savannah that connects the cheetahs to the zebras, where you can walk through the tall grass and imagine what it's like to be hunting antelope. The only cheetah I spot is asleep, under a rock dome, oblivious to the striped prey prancing on the other side of a metal fence. Presumably, back in Africa, they would have made an excellent dinner. Here, the cheetahs get fed twice a day, and all they have to do is walk to the gray house when the keepers come around. I wouldn't tell the kid that.

Eva walks up the path wearing a new sweater. It's blue. She also has a new pair of jeans on and her hair is down. Her hands are in her pocket.

"Hi," she says.

"Hey."

"I told you I'd clean up," she says.

"I have your key."

She doesn't say anything for a while, then her face softens into something like hope.

"Did you go in?" she says softly.

"No."

She takes one hand out of her pocket and puts it on my shoulder. My body tightens and she pulls her hand away.

"Do you want to sit somewhere?" she says.

Something is different today. She's not even mad I didn't go in.

"Actually, I would rather walk."

"Okay. Where do you want to go?" she asks.

"I don't know. You probably know this place better than I do."

"Probably. We used to come here a lot."

I think she means with her mother, but I know better than to ask. Not right now. We pass the pandas and head down the hill, but they've closed off the house where the hippo and the elephants used to live.

"I don't know where they've put the hippo," Eva says. "Pablo loved him. We'd wait for him to come up and snort and laugh our asses off. My mom was the best at making animal noises. She did the best elephant."

I nod and swerve around a bulldozer, past the small mammals to the back of the ape house. The gorillas aren't out today. It's too cold for them.

"Can we go in here?" I ask, already pushing the back door.

Eva nods.

"Sure," she says. "I love the gorillas."

We're doing the exhibit backwards, but there's no one here to get on our case. The orangutans are looking especially shaggy, picking fleas out of each other's hair, neck, and elbows. One of them has a gaping wound on his neck that makes me look away. It reminds me of the hole in the Irish singer's guitar. Each time the orangutan swings from one branch to the other, the scar opens up a little, but nothing falls out, and nothing seems to be back there. It's just an open, flappy wound. I wish someone would tell me what happened to him.

"That's Mandara," Eva says, pointing to the gorillas in their indoor playgrounds. "Over there. She's the super-mom."

A long, black, hairy arm hangs loose from the side of a hammock, and the fingers scrape the floor from time to time. I follow the arm to a shoulder, then a long face with sad, peaceful eyes. As we approach the glass, Mandara turns around and gives us her back. A tiny gorilla climbs over her waist to the other side. I had missed the baby before.

"That's Kibibi," Eva says. "It means little girl. She was born last year, to one of the silverback boys chewing over there."

I count four other gorillas. Most of them are eating. They sit down on their heels and then shuffle around and sit again.

"How do you know all this stuff?"

Eva shrugs. "I like animals."

I nod.

"They're comforting, you know. They don't break your balls. They don't need much. They just do their thing, no questions, no bullshit."

"I guess," I say.

When the silverback moves, the others get out of his way. He looks bored to me, unchallenged in his cage.

"It doesn't make you a little sad?" I ask.

"What?" Eva says, her eyes fixed on the scene behind the glass.

"I don't know. That they're captive and stuff," I say.

Eva laughs.

"I hate to break it to you, but we're a lot more captive than they are. Look at her," she says, pointing to the mother gorilla. "Does she look worried to you?"

I stand on my toes to look at Kibibi and her mother again. The little one is sucking on her mother's breast, and her fingers are spread over the dark brown chest. Mandara, the mother, is neither bothered nor endeared—she just is.

Eva is right. If I were a gorilla, I wouldn't have any of these issues. I wouldn't have choices. It would all just be instinct. I would eat, or I would starve. I would mate, or I would sleep. I would live, or I would die. That's it. No rituals—no funerals, no baby showers, no prayers. No art, no music.

It's gotten so bad, I can't decide if I'd rather be a gorilla.

"Are you ready to go?" Eva sounds impatient now. She's found a bench and is staring at the rubbery plants in the foyer.

I'd like to stay a little longer, but I can tell her mood is changing, so I follow her and try to work up the courage to confess that I don't have a new picture. I am here because she asked me to come. I'm here for her. Because I have her key in my pocket and her book in my bag, and because I want to know her story, since I'm now a part of it. She is Picasso, and I pushed her over. It's my work to lift her back up.

I look up at the wires hanging over our heads for the orangutans to swing around on.

"Do your parents know about this?" Eva says suddenly.

"About the pictures?"

"About us."

She's looking at her shoes. I notice she's not wearing any socks.

"They don't," I say.

Eva nods.

"Why do you want to know?" I ask.

"Never mind."

"What?" I insist.

"Did they tell you not to come or something?" she says, her eyes on something too far away for me to see.

"I told you. They don't know."

"Okay, I got it. I thought you might be close to your parents."

"I am," I say.

"Okay, good, I just—"

"What makes you think I'm not? What makes you think they would want to know? I'm taking pictures of your house, so what? You basically blackmailed me."

It all comes out fast, probably to flood the thing I'm afraid to say.

"I didn't blackmail you." She sounds upset. "You agreed to take the pictures."

I bite my lip and breathe. I think of all the times I could have dropped out, from the planetarium to the house key, and how I always chose to go on. Maybe this is my fate, like Eva said on the first day. Whether in the Book of Life or the Book of the Dead, our names are written right next to each other. Eva and Miriam. Picasso and Paloma.

"You wanted to take the pictures," Eva says softly, as if reading my thoughts.

"Maybe," I say, "but I still don't know why."

"Because you can," she says.

"What about you?"

"What do you mean?" she asks.

"You wouldn't even have to take pictures. You could just walk right through that front door. Use your own key."

I put my hand in my pocket, but I don't take it out yet.

"You don't know what you're talking about," she says, grimacing.

"You said so yourself. Everybody's there. What are you doing here?"

"Watch the way you talk to me," she hisses. "The real reason your parents don't know about me is because you were too scared to tell them about the Picasso."

I try to imagine the strongest thing I know. The ocean comes up first, but I'd rather picture something solid, something that stands still. I see the locust tree in Adam's backyard. I am the locust tree, I think. She cannot move me. Eva sighs.

"Let me see the picture," she says.

My spine grows longer.

"Please show me the picture," she says.

"I don't have anything," I say.

She examines my face with her usual intensity.

"You're lying," she says.

I'm breathing short, thick breaths. Tree breaths. My tongue pushes hard against my teeth.

"I don't lie," I say.

"We know that's not true," she says.

"Not to you," I say.

"But I asked you to please get a picture of Pablo," she pleads. "I gave you a key."

"I couldn't," I say.

"Why not?" she says.

"I was carving a pumpkin with my mother," I say, as serious as I can be.

She looks up like she's thinking hard, or trying hard not to think.

"That sounds nice," she says.

"It was," I say, surprised at how true that is, and how quickly she changed her tone.

"I loved my mother too," she says.

"You don't love her anymore?"

She looks horrified.

"Of course I do," she says.

"Sorry," I say.

"It's okay. It's just sometimes it's not enough to love people."

"I know," I say. "But you should go home."

And then again, "Go home."

Eva starts crying. A lot. Silent, but a shit ton. Massive tears.

"You don't know," she says.

"It's okay," I say.

"It's not."

"Eva."

"You don't know what it's like."

"What?" I ask. "What?"

We're stalled in front of the reptile house. A few kids are

leaning over the rail looking for the alligator, but he's well hidden. I can't believe this is how I'm going to leave her.

"Don't you want to see them all in real life, not in some pictures I took?"

"Are you going to take a picture?"

"Did you just leave, Eva?"

"I did," she says. "I left. And now I don't know how to go back."

"Why?"

"Because I'm scared of what I did."

"What did you do?"

"I got so mad."

"You got mad? That's why you left?"

"I couldn't keep up with everything. Everything was changing. I was yelling a lot, and then promising not to yell, and then yelling again. I couldn't stop. I was just mad."

"What were you so mad about? Who were you yelling at?"

Eva sighs.

"What happened?"

I can feel the pull again now, the force of your life happening to you, the pull of our story, mine and hers.

"One morning, he wouldn't get out of his pajamas, you know, to have breakfast. And I was so tired."

"Pablo?"

"Yes. I don't have to tell this story if you don't want to hear it."

"I want to know. I need to know."

"Well, he kept asking if he could just eat breakfast in

his pajamas, and I kept telling him no, and explaining why. He kept promising he wouldn't spill anything, and that he would eat really quickly. I wanted to say yes, but I couldn't. I couldn't. I told him no and he screamed. I told him to be quiet and he yelled louder, right in my face.

"So I told him to be quiet again and go into his room, and he stomped his foot and he pushed me away. I grabbed him and put him in his room and told him to stop it, and he yelled more and more until my *tía* came in to see what was wrong. He just kept saying *ayudame, ayudame, help me, help me*, but I didn't. I kept telling him he could do it himself. He ran down to the kitchen, and I just ran after him, yelling at the top of my lungs. He had the juice carton in his hands and he was getting ready to pour some, and I told him to put it back. He said *NO*. And then I just lost it. I hit him right across the face. Hard, Miriam. Right on his temple."

She's wiping the tears with her palm, but her voice is so steady, it's as if the story and the tears aren't even connected.

"He screamed so loud, I grabbed him again. Then I could see his little face getting scared, and I felt so horrible, but I couldn't let go of his arms. He pulled, and I let go, and he hit the floor."

I don't know what to say, but I can tell she's waiting for something.

"Did you say you were sorry?" I ask.

"Yes, and he just went on up the stairs and we put his clothes on. He lifted his feet to fit them through his pants. His cheek was swollen. I knew it would bruise. I could almost see it turning red, then purple, then yellow. I did that. But he was so quiet. He let me rinse his face with the washcloth, pull the dinosaur shirt right over his head. He didn't say a thing. I told him it wasn't nice to hit, and that you should never do it no matter how mad you are. He didn't really respond. He just went downstairs and asked me for milk."

"Okay, well then, it sounds like he forgave you, like everything was okay. Did you get in trouble? Was your mom pissed?"

My comment seems to amuse her slightly.

"He didn't forgive me. He just went on. Because I'm big, and he's only a little boy. I always thought I would protect him,"

"That's good."

"Yes, it's good, but I hurt him instead."

"You're his sister. Sisters do that sometimes," I say.

She looks at me and shakes her head.

"I'm sure everybody loses it. Doesn't your mom yell at him?"

"My mother never yelled at anybody," she says.

Her face twists into disgust, like she's smelling something awful.

"She never even raised her voice."

Neither did mine, or I can't remember if she did. She pushed my legs off the back of the passenger seat once, and then handed me crayons before I could cry.

"I'm going to do it again," she says. "Once you do it once, you just do it again."

The tears are still coming, but the wiping has turned to

scrubbing, her face a stubborn pot. I reach over and grab her wrist.

"Stop," I say. "Your mom is there."

"My mom is not there," she says.

"But she is," I say. "She'll get better, won't she?"

She doesn't say anything.

"Look, I wouldn't push the sculpture again," I say. "I learned from my mistake."

Eva jerks her hand away and reaches for the empty space around her waist. She grabs the end of her sweater and stretches it down toward her thighs.

"You don't know, Miriam. You don't know the feeling right after you do something like that. I know he got up. I know I love him. But I broke it. I broke something. I destroyed something. It was something, and then it wasn't anymore. I destroyed it. I did that. It was safe and then it wasn't. It was love and then it wasn't. How could that be love? How could he believe me when I say that to him now?"

She looks away for a minute, catching her breath, considering her own dilemma. This seems like too much for a sister to take on.

"It was a mistake," I say.

She shakes her head. "Maybe," she says. "But you can't go back. You can't come back after some mistakes."

I'd like to say that isn't true, but I am not convinced. After all, I pushed the statue and I still haven't told anyone. I lied to my parents. If I ever come back, I don't know who it is they're getting.

"You're probably right," I say.

"So then what am I supposed to do?" she says, a little aggressive.

I think about my parents. I think about Elliot. I see Adam in front of me, his shoulders, his neck, his grin. I want to destroy them all, but most of all, I want them to survive. As I picture that, I remember the statue, and how good it felt to push her, when she was still strong, before she fell over. How right it seemed to lean against her, to stun her out of her peace. I can see her looking at me like that, without eyes or a real face, looking like me looking at her, looking like me covered in bronze. I get it, I should say to Eva. I get why you hit your brother. But the words are stuck in the place where we manufacture them, rolling off the assembly line, making mischief in the room of my thoughts. Eva looks like she forgot the question.

"You know when people say they can't stand something?" I say.

"Yeah."

"What do you think they mean, exactly?" I ask.

"I don't know. That they can't take it, I guess. That they don't know how to take it."

"Right. I agree."

"What are you trying to say?" she asks.

"That it's not about hating something."

"Is this about the sculpture?" she says.

I am not sure what it's about.

"When something is precious," I try, "people are always telling you to be careful with it, so you try to be. And that works for a vase or an antique, but not with a person."

She is not looking at me, but she's listening. I can tell.

"Because you can never really get close when you're too scared to hurt someone. So, you should. Or maybe you shouldn't. But we do."

"Do what?" she says, releasing one hand and switching to the other.

"Hurt each other," I say.

She turns her head. I see the puzzle on her face. I want to make her understand.

"So he knows you're not perfect, so that you can survive it, so that it can all be real. Sometimes you can't stand love, so you have to hurt it."

That doesn't make sense, but it feels exactly true. The words mean something I can't understand yet. The words are doing their job without me, and I will just have to catch up later.

"So that you can actually love someone and they can love you," I say, "even if you weren't careful, even if you weren't kind, even if you were exposed as the mean, selfish, ugly-ass thing that you are."

She stares.

"Did you read that in a book?" she asks.

"Maybe," I say, because everything comes from some-where, right, and it may as well be a book.

She releases both hands from her sweater and rubs her knees with her palms. There's a faint smile growing on her lips. It has a patronizing slant.

"Is that what you think you are?" she asks softly, but with a strange confidence.

"What?"

"A mean, selfish, ugly-ass thing?"

"I don't know," I say, trying not to blush.

"Thank you for the pictures," she says.

I shrug.

"You may be right about all this stuff," she says, "but you never really lost anything."

A rush of heat fills my face, a flood of shame.

"Maybe not," I say, "but it feels like I did."

We sit there and watch the visitors roll by. A lion roars, somewhere farther away than it sounds. A boy runs to grab his father's leg. They laugh. People let their children throw bread to the turtles in the pond. The keepers pretend not to see it. The silence between us is heavy, but I feel lighter. Everything is in relief. Eva suddenly stands and walks to a bench in front of the souvenir store. Two men beside us are weaving fake spiderwebs around a tree, debating what branches to dangle them from. Eva doesn't see the men. She's staring straight ahead. Her face is blotchy from all the crying.

"I'm such a fucking whiner," she says. "I'm sorry."

"That's okay. I'm just not sure what to do. Do you need something?"

"Maybe some water would help," she says.

"Okay. I can get that."

I stand and look around for a vending machine. "Give me a minute. I'll be right back."

"Miriam?"

"Yes?"

"Every day I'm out here, it gets harder and harder to go back."

I give her a quick look of solidarity, take out my wallet, and drop my tote on the bench as a security deposit, to show her I'm not leaving her.

Eva nods quietly and I head back up the hill. I'm going to find what this girl needs. I'm going to go back there. I'm going to take care of one thing at a time. I find a machine that asks for two fifty for a bottle of water. I slip the money into the slot and punch the blue logo.

The bathrooms are right next door, so I run in there. I wash my hands and steal a look at my face. Is it rounder? Is it tired? Then I remember the water, Eva, the bench. Focus.

When I get back, my bag is sitting right where I left it, but she's not there. I look around at the fake waterfall and the kids huddled around to feed the turtles they're not supposed to feed. No new sweater, no shiny hair. I head for the big cats, but she's not there either. All I find is a tiger, pacing back and forth on the edge of the water. Wanting out.

At the bottom of the hill, there's an exit and a big clock that's stuck at 11:45. I look for my phone. It's actually four-thirty. The walk back up the hill to my bike is unbearable: the hill is especially steep, and my breath is short from looking for Eva. The cheetahs are still napping. When I get to my bike, I call Eva and it goes straight to voicemail. That's Pablo saying the numbers. So you hit your brother, Eva. What makes you think he's better off without you? *I'm going to do it again,* she said. I take out the phone and text her.

i have your water.

Erase that.

where are you?

On the way home, the wind threatens to throw me off the bike a few times, especially on the way up from Connecticut Ave, past the zombies and jack-o'-lanterns and poisonous plastic spiders. I stop at the top of the hill to rearrange my school stuff and switch sides. Bogart is gone. She took my camera.

# TWENTY-NINE

At home, someone is upstairs in my room. Probably Mom sorting laundry, but my night pictures are still up there somewhere, so I should check. When I open the door, Adam is sitting cross-legged reading my library book. That Adam. That library book. He's in the middle of it, his hands over someone's blue face. Adam found my Picasso book. I want to scream, but my body won't let me, it's had so much. I squeeze the door handle so I can stay in between. His toes peek out from under his knees, and he's wearing one of those nameless, shapeless shirts guys can wear their whole lives. The kind that comes in a pack of ten.

"So, apparently . . . " he says as he turns the pages, "Picasso liked sad women."

His voice is comforting, but my body is frozen in fear. He doesn't look up, and I can see the place where the barber shaves his neck under the curls, that dip in the neck, that tiny, empty pond. I could spit in it. His shoulder bones poke out under the T-shirt, sharper than when we were twelve-year-old boy and girl.

"*Young Girl Struck By Sadness*, 1939. *Young Tormented Girl*, 1939. Lots of young girls. I guess he liked them. Basically, the guy got a wife or a mistress every time he wanted to paint somebody new. This Olga portrait is outstanding, with her arm draped over the chair like that ... the face like an egg, the eyes. She's so serious."

"I got your pictures," I say. "Or my pictures. Thank you."

"You're welcome," he says. "I figured, when you came by the other day ... "

Adam's voice is uneven. He's afraid I might interrupt. He wants me to listen. I take my hand off the knob and look around at my ocean.

"There's just so much color in these," he says. "Colors you'd have to make up in the real world. And shapes. It's so fucking weird, but it works. I can see why you like it. You got this from the library, right? I didn't know you liked Picasso. You've been talking about him lately, but I didn't know you liked him. I get it."

It doesn't seem like Adam cares if I talk or not. He smiles and shakes his head, and turns quickly through the pages where the faces stare back, deformed, a nightmare of faces. I wonder how long he's known.

"This one looks like you," he says, pointing to a drawing,

maybe pencil or pen, of Françoise, one of Picasso's favorite mistresses. She's beautiful.

"How long have you known?" I whisper.

"From the beginning," he says.

He swallows and pushes his hair off his face.

"She's got your lips."

Adam looks up and straight into my eyes and does not move, the book still open in his lap. That's when I know this is not a game. We've played well. We've made our moves. We've delivered all of our lines. We've been good friends and good partners. We've had our little lovely life. Now is where he's asking me something, and what we have to do next is, we have to dissolve. This is how this one ends. I walk over to Adam, take the book from his hand and place it flat and open on the carpet—face down. When I look back up, his eyes are still on mine. He is braver than I imagined, braver than I made him out to be.

He pulls at my sweater, with unexpected force, until our faces are close enough to breathe on, but not close enough to recognize. My fingers look for the dip at the nape of his neck, and we kiss and think of nothing and everything, of teeth and photographs, of snow and warm chests, of muscles and spines. His hands reach under my shirt, and the fingers spread at the bottom of my back to pull me even closer. My legs start to ache from kneeling like this, but I'm afraid to change position, afraid of what we might look like when we pull apart.

Adam does not seem afraid at all. His mouth is on my

face and my neck and my ears, his curls trailing after him, tickling everything he kisses. Our bodies become more frantic, less careful and less loving, closer, more hungry. I have not been kissed in a thousand years. I stop him.

"Hey," he says, looking at me.

"Hey."

"Are you okay?" he says.

"Yeah, but we shouldn't."

"You don't want to?"

"I can't right now," I say.

"I love you, Miriam," he says. "I really do."

"I know, Adam."

"Good."

He moves close, and I'm afraid he's going to kiss me again, but instead he rests his chin on my shoulder.

"I don't want to leave," he says.

"You have to," I answer.

He looks a little concerned. I'm too warm to feel the chill of what we've done, and when he stands up, I close my eyes so I won't have to look. He's not my old friend anymore. Already, he's not. He gives me a kiss on the cheek, and his lazy eye stays lazy a little longer than usual. I don't tease him.

"I'm going, but I'm not going," he says.

"Okay."

"Are you … ?"

"I'm good, Adam."

"Good," he says, and he walks out without his bag or his jacket, without even closing the book. My hands smell like him. My hair smells like him. My neck smells like him. My wrists smell like him.

Under the covers, I escape into sleep and me and Malcolm X are together on a sailboat and he is telling me everything, everything I need to know. He's giving me all the answers, but I can't seem to remember any of it (it all just slips away) and I'm looking for my camera, because I want to take a picture of him (because I'm in a boat with Malcolm X), but I can't find it anywhere and it's night and he's not there anymore and now we're in a courtyard where there's one chair and all these leaves are everywhere, rotting. On one side of the courtyard, Elliot is cooking an omelette, and I can see him through his window, but when I look back at the chair, Adam is sitting on it, and he tells me to sit on his lap, which I do, but I'm still looking at Elliot. I can't wait to tell Elliot I just saw Malcolm X, but he won't lift his head away from the pan and I can never see his face. I can't make eye contact. I can't get his attention. I don't remember what he looks like.

I wake up choking on my breath. The street lights are on outside. My door is shut. The house is quiet. My eyes adjust to find my cell phone: 1:10 a.m. One new text, from Adam.

Good night, Meem. Wanna ride the bus
   tomorrow?

There's a handwritten note near my phone:

*We tried to wake you up but it was impossible.*
*Leftovers in the fridge.*

*See you tomorrow.*

I walk into the bathroom to pee and check if my parents' light is still on. The only noise is the rinse cycle in the dishwasher downstairs. They must have stayed up later than usual. I brush my teeth and rinse my mouth out to get rid of the nightmare taste.

Back in bed, I go through my third grade roster, alphabetically. I sing "You Are My Sunshine" in my head five times. I count the number of years Henri Cartier-Bresson lived. When I get to ninety-six, I take time to remember my mom's birthday present. I was fourteen. She gave me a copy of *The Decisive Moment,* Cartier-Bresson's book. Her dedication is scribbled under the title, on the first page:

*Cartier-Bresson was not interested in the darkroom.*
*Don't spend all your time in there. The viewfinder*
*is where you make your pictures. The world is where*
*you get them. Get out there.*

*Love, Mom.*

I stole that line from my mother so many times. *The viewfinder is where you make your pictures.* I've spit it at Adam whenever he wanted to crop a picture, make it brighter, or highlight the most important detail.

Even evil David was impressed with my plagiarized

thought over wine, cheese, and blue grapes. Yes, we sixteen-year-olds drank wine at Elliot's house. We were sophisticated there, an odd kind of progressive, at least about wine. *Well said, Miriam. What a smart girl you found, Elliot. And not afraid to have an opinion.* Elliot had winked at me. Bear with it, his eyes seemed to say. Eventually, we will sleep together and laugh about this. But I *am* smart, I had wanted to tell everybody in the room. This isn't a joke. I'm not being cute.

I get up and look for *The Decisive Moment* in the boxes in my closet. I've marked my favorite parts with little exploding snowflakes.

*"Photography is simultaneously and instantaneously the recognition of a fact,"* Cartier-Bresson wrote, *"and the rigorous organization of visually perceived forms that express and signify that fact."*

So that's what I am. I'm a photographer struggling to recognize a series of facts. And staying awake isn't going to help. I need sleep to think straight, and I need to think straight to get sleep. My jeans are crumpled on the floor. I crack the window open and stick my hands out to read the temperature.

Elliot's socks are still under my bed, and Adam's camera beckons from the floor. He forgot it here this afternoon. The screen is printed with the lines of his thumbs, like sweaty tree circles telling time. I put the strap around my neck, like a tourist. The body of the camera falls right in the middle of my chest, the lens looking out to lead me through the dark house. Now Adam's name is in the book too. We are all tangled.

The wind is brutal, and it almost knocks me off the

bike once or twice. It's not constant, more like gusts, and I can't predict when the next one will come. I turn onto the main arteries, hoping that the bigger buildings will shield me better. I ride past many of our regular haunts: the coffee place, the movie theater, the water tower at Fort Reno.

Everything in the store windows looks trapped. The oranges, the hula hoops, the power drill and leather boots; the televisions, the laundry hampers, the antique chair; the milk steamers and the cold medicine and the composition notebooks, they are all sleeping behind the shatterproof glass. All the objects look so discouraged, as if they dread the impending fluorescent light that will get them handled, kidnapped, and consumed.

There is a great little stream of nervous energy in my insomnia. Despite the wind, the slopes feel possible tonight. My body is drawn to this place; I couldn't get lost if I tried. A rush of something cool quenches my sleepless, beat-up body. On Elliot's street, the lamps turn everything orange. I drop my bike on the sidewalk several feet back from the front door. The neighborhood wind chimes clank furiously.

Adam's camera is in "open" view.

Most of the lights are off, except for the desk lamp in his room. I refuse to think of Elliot, in his bed under his sheets, but in refusing, I picture it perfectly. To wake him or not to wake him. I set up the tripod on the slippery grass. Adam's camera fits perfectly, of course. I just need to breathe and click, and then we're done. It's all ready, but I wait.

What would you do if you were sitting in front of your

sleeping ex's house, feeling like you had very little love left, but still so much longing? How would you lock up all that nostalgia? For me, it's a picture. It always is, and always will be. You don't shut it out. You lock it up and take it with you. I know that now.

Someone walks into his room. I gasp and look closer, squinting my eyes in the dark. It's his mother, in her pajamas. I'm embarrassed to see her like this. Even in Delaware this summer, she was always dressed by breakfast. I grab the tripod, leave the camera on, and take a few steps back.

She walks toward Elliot's bed, stops, looks, steps back toward the desk, and extends her arm to flick the light off. I don't see her leaving the room or closing the door, and I can't hear her saying good night or I love you. Do mothers still do that? I don't have a picture yet.

As I get ready to leave, her own bathroom light comes on, across the house. Mrs. Fox pulls her hair up, splashes her face, and brushes her teeth. This is the picture I take, as she gets ready to go to bed. The wind comes back suddenly, and a loud thump makes me run to the bike. I get on and lean into the wind, to make a U-turn. A giant rodent is crawling across Elliot's lawn. He's huge. He looks lost. He is shaking, like he's scared, and dragging his tail along the dying grass. I ride back past the house without looking in.

Pedaling back home, I resolve to meet Elliot outside of school, like I did almost two years ago. I have three hours before the alarm clock goes off again, so in anticipation of the force with which my head will hit the pillow, I try Eva again.

> I went to the guy's house. I think the wind knocked
> a possum out of his tree. Is it a sign?

After I read it over the third time, the message strikes me as a metaphor I can't understand, and that thought gives me peace. That's the last feeling I have before I fall asleep: a sliver of pure peace.

# THIRTY

Adam is in the student lounge, which is essentially a glass box, but he doesn't see me. He's wearing a sweater I've never seen before. He's talking to Victor, probably about photographs, and his hands are drawing something monstrous in the air. I already feel like I've betrayed him. Victor notices me first and motions through the glass for me to join them. Adam smiles a brave, handsome smile and my fingers feel shaky down there, at the tip of my body.

Actually, it feels like every extremity could just drop off, starting with my fingers, then my hair, then all the teeth in my mouth. I'm losing to the floor. Adam's face shifts from brave to scared, and he walks toward the door, toward me. The rest of the room fades, the kids and their laptops are all little dots in an impressionist painting. I back into a wall and lean while the room pirouettes giddily—my Adam, my fixed point.

"Hey," he says.

His eyes are softer than they were yesterday, less determined.

"Does Victor know?" I say.

His face scrunches, betraying surprise and disgust in equal measure. I see how easily I can hurt him, how easily I can make him afraid.

"What do you mean?" he says.

"It looks like he knows. Does Victor know what happened yesterday?"

As the words come out, I suck all those lost pieces back into me. My body is whole in rage. Aggression glues it back together.

"No. Of course not."

"Good. I don't want him to know."

Victor has stopped at the door. He can tell we are talking about something important. He waves and sits back down on the fake leather couches. Adam is probably telling the truth. Victor probably doesn't know.

"Did you get my message?" Adam asks.

"Yes. My dad took me to school."

He looks away to think for a second. "Oh. Cool."

"It has nothing to do with you."

"No, I know. It's nice."

My heart is like playdough left out overnight. Crusty. Someone should throw it out already. Adam is struggling.

"Why are you so far away, Miriam?"

He reaches out for my hand, in the middle of the hallway, in front of every hungry beast in the student lounge. I let him have it, but I don't squeeze back. After a few seconds, he lets go, and I put it in my pocket, where I feel for Eva's key. It's not there. I can't remember if I left it under the pillow last night. Or in my other pocket. Maybe yesterday's jeans.

"Are you scared?" he asks.

I snicker. "You have no idea."

"I'm scared too, Miriam, but we have to stick together. Like Robert Frank and Allen Ginsberg. Like James Agee and Walker Evans. Like Bogart and Bacall."

I don't tell him Bogart's gone, or that I used his camera to take a picture of Elliot's house last night. I try to sneak out of his gaze, away to join the other bodies dragging or bouncing to class. To look for my key. I just want to find the key, then I can talk to him.

"Can we just talk? Will you walk home with me? I think we need to talk and figure this out," he says, sounding urgent.

That last part makes me squirm, because there's nothing like a boy saying what he should be saying when you are trying to blame him for what's making you sick. I need to go now.

"Okay," I say quickly.

"Okay," he says, not moving.

"I gotta go to class," I say.

"Okay. I'll see you after school."

"Fine."

"Main gate."

"Okay."

I walk to the bathroom and realize no one's life has been altered by our exchange. Victor welcomes Adam back into

209

their conversation. The hall is still full of smart boys and girls planning how to drink themselves dumb. To them, it's just Miriam and Adam talking, the photo freaks, best friends since Torah school. But I remember last night and his face when he took off my shirt. I recognized those eyes. Hope and fear together make hunger. That's it. That's the one feeling in the world. Hunger. I was wanted, people. Wake up. I was loved.

# THIRTY-ONE

I need my camera.

all my pictures are in there.

can you just answer me?

you can drop it off wherever you want.

are you okay?

i still have your key.

# THIRTY~TWO

I consider getting a late pass from Ms. K, but I don't want to step into her talking trap right now. When I walk into Calculus late and sans excuse, Mr. L lets it slide because I do my homework every night, and occasionally ask useful questions. The only empty seat is next to Maggie Sawyer.

Maggie is pretty, but not scary pretty. She is funny, but not side splitting witty, never sarcastic. She knows when to talk and when to be quiet. She can negotiate with boys. She has friends who play tennis and friends who play guitar. She reads her Austen and her *Cosmo*. She's balanced, very very balanced.

So balanced she flashes me an empathetic smile when I duck into the chair and promise myself I will get through these forty-five minutes. After seventeen years of grooming, at my mother's imagined insistence, I smile back the most polite smile I can muster.

The class is in the middle of Mr. Lang's practice exercises, and I pull out my pencil to catch up. It feels smooth and familiar. I hold it under my nose. It smells like second grade.

"Do you want to look at my notes, Miriam?"

Her voice always sounds like she's got strep throat, which I imagine Elliot finds sexy, because I do, begrudgingly.

"Uhm, thanks. Sure."

She slides her notebook across our joined desks, motioning for me to keep it on my side of the line. She's in no hurry. I look around to confirm what I suspected. Everyone is looking at us. This interaction makes for great gossip, since everyone knows Elliot and I were practically married last year, and that it's Maggie he's swapping spit with now. According to the general public, there was a grace period of about two months when Elliot belonged to nobody but himself.

What they don't know is he came to see me in the dog days of August. About two weeks before school started, when the city returns to its swampy origins, the mosquitoes come up with the sun, and the air conditioning doubles you over at the grocery store. My parents were at work. Adam was on his annual family vacation out West, in big sky country, channeling his inner fly-fisherman. I was debating whether to throw out every picture of Elliot I'd ever taken. Our low, limited sky was begging to release, like a kid who can't find a bathroom. It wanted to rain.

Elliot rang the doorbell, and I answered and let him in, like I had in every single one of my daydreams since Delaware. He looked as sad as he had in the best of them, as ashamed and desperate as I hoped he would. If I'd kept my mouth shut, if we had stayed in that doorway, he would've been mine forever.

The minute I told him to come inside, I started losing, leaking power and confidence, washing the floors with my resolutions.

"Can I sit?" he said.

"Sure."

"I haven't been here in so long," he said.

"It's not that long. You want something to eat?"

"Just water or something."

I took my time in the kitchen, so he would think about me more. I was wearing Mom's yoga pants and a tank top. I considered changing and decided not to. Too desperate. Too obvious. I took off my bra instead, and temporarily hid it in the spice cabinet, behind the cumin and the turmeric and the five-pepper steak mix. Nothing is pre-meditated. Nothing is for a reason. *Everything is a decisive moment.* We do things because we do things. And then sometimes we deal with what we've done. Sometimes.

I poured Elliot a glass of orange juice. When I came back, he was looking at one of my baby pictures, smiling at what he'd lost. It was perfect. I could not have written a better script.

"You could tell you were stubborn back then too," he said.

"Oh yeah?"

"Yes, all that hair and your smile. Like you're not scared of anything."

I barely acknowledged him, but inside my head the redemption orchestra played a full house. I tried to focus on keeping him at arm's length, where he could look and not touch.

"So, what are you doing here?"

Sigh. Slouch. Green eyes up.

"I'm sorry."

"Well, you can always leave," says the girl whose bra is in the spice cabinet.

"I'm not sorry I'm here. I'm sorry about what happened in Delaware."

He looks invigorated, like this is the part of the speech he remembers well, like it's coming back to him.

"I know we haven't talked in a couple of weeks, and that you probably don't want anything to do with me, but I just wanted to see you again. I have these nightmares."

"Me too."

"Yeah?" he says, hope lighting up his eyes.

"Yes. It's hard to go to sleep."

"What do you dream about?"

I shake my head.

"Am I in them? Am I in your dreams?" he asked.

"It's none of your business."

"I guess not," he says. "In mine, you're always behind a camera, and I keep telling you to take it away from your face so I can see you, but you won't, and I never do. I never see your face. It drives me nuts."

Now that I know what I know, now that I've finally bled, now that I kissed my best friend, maybe the only real friend I have left now, I think that this part may have been a lie, because nobody's nightmares make that much sense. Dreams are weirder, much messier than that. There's got to be an octopus that is trying to have sex with you, or a policeman telling you that you can't go to the snow mobile ball, or your mother with red monster eyes. Shit that makes you uncomfortable, stuff you don't want to repeat. Not me hiding behind a camera lens and you wanting to see my face. That's too perfect.

Never mind hindsight, though, because after the dream story is exactly when I turned around and walked up to my room, and he put down his half-drunk orange juice and followed me. When we got inside, he saw the ocean walls and didn't say a word. He just took off my clothes and kissed me. Everywhere he could reach. We stuck together and repelled like magnets in a kid's hands until the warmth of victory and recognition and desire kicked in, and I swallowed up all my righteousness for one, last, sweet time.

Against the wall, I could still smell the paint, the latest coat a few days fresh. To this day, I sometimes put my nose up to it, but whatever has happened since has dulled the smell. I clung on like a barnacle to a ship as he took his clothes off, and, my body being human and not holy, I gave in with great pleasure and hope. I like to think we both did, from whatever heights we had been standing on.

We didn't use a condom. This is the part where I should say we were drunk, or stupid, or didn't have time to think.

That would be lying. I knew one of the thousand sperms could make it to one of my numbered eggs and that could mean the thing that didn't end up happening. I had been told, and I had been warned, and up until then I had been safe, and smart, and honest. But the thing I wanted was for him to want me. So maybe we could have had a baby. But nobody had explained to me how or why I should refuse the chance to feel whole again. I didn't know what I wanted to be when I grew up. All I wanted was for us to be enough to cover everything, from here until there.

Every moment after that was a little more dirt on the grave, until the day I knocked over the sculpture, when my body kicked my mind into gear and I could not hide anymore. That August afternoon, we slept until the heat got unbearable and we both had to shower. I tried hard not to say anything, but when Elliot came out of the bathroom, I could tell he had been crying.

"What's wrong?" I said.

"Nothing."

"You look upset."

"It's nothing, Miriam."

"All right. I was just asking because you ... "

"Look, I'm glad I came," he said.

That particular brick is still lodged in my chest.

"Whoa, well, I hope so."

"I came to say I was sorry about the way I acted. At the house. With my father and you."

"I know. I get it. Why are you upset right now? I feel like you're mad at me."

"I'm not mad. I just don't want anybody to get hurt anymore."

Ring. The. Alarm.

"Get hurt?"

"I don't know, Miriam."

"I'm sorry, I don't understand you right now. Are you saying you wish we hadn't…"

"No. That's not it."

"Well, what are you saying, Elliot?"

"I don't know. Just forget it."

I wish I had wanted to pick him up and throw him against the wall, then kick him hard, a hundred thousand times. Right as he was putting his clothes back on, when he wouldn't see it coming. I wish I had wanted to hurt him, but all I wanted was *yes*. One, unmistakable *yes*.

"Do you love me?" I said, trying my best not to sound whiny.

"Of course."

"Are you in love with me?"

He looked away. "I don't know, Miriam. I don't know."

Thank God he kissed my wet hair and left right then, because I would have actually tried to make my case. Really. Nobody likes to take no for an answer, but "maybe" is even worse. It's nothing. He left me with nothing except for his socks, which is the only thing I can hold over Maggie Sawyer.

"Do you need Monday's notes too?" Maggie asks, all timid, but loud enough for our neighbors to hear.

I shake my head. "That's okay."

"Are you sure? It's all right with me. I don't even look at my notes half the time."

"I'm all right," I say. "Thank you."

"I didn't mean I don't *need* the notes. I do. I'm just so bad with math. Sometimes I don't even want to look at it."

I scan the notes for any evidence that would support her cute self-deprecation. The writing is neat. The pages are supple. I am sure she looks at the notes, does her homework, and gets it right at least eighty-percent of the time. She's just good at making herself smaller, so you have more room to feel important. It's disarming. I will give her that. I hand the notes back.

"Thanks," I say.

"Not a problem. If you ever miss class and need crappy notes, you know where to find them."

I cock my head a little. "Thanks, but I don't plan on missing class."

She looks away and bites her pink tongue. "I didn't mean that you do."

"Look, I don't care. Don't worry about it."

"You just missed some classes this week, so … "

"I missed some classes, and now I'm back. Thank you so much for your notes. They're not at all crappy, and I'm not at all offended."

She turns a little red, in uneven blotches, which immediately makes me feel better until I think of Adam, who is waiting for me at the main gate.

"Good," she says, finally. "Good."

It occurs to me that Maggie Sawyer will never know I could have been pregnant with her boyfriend's child, that he doesn't even have to know, that it doesn't even matter anymore. I'm not. As Maggie Sawyer writes numbers in her notebook, I see how easy it is to be around her, how much more humble and understanding she is. How much lighter.

Adam's last class is French, on the third floor, almost directly above me. When the bell rings, I can't think of a better place to hide than Ms. K's office, where she opens the door and looks surprised. I have no plan, so I spend the first twenty minutes talking about the photo assignment and how it's going, throwing in an apology or two for my mother's outburst and for skipping class. Ms. K is pleased with my improvised enthusiasm, and she takes it as an invitation to ask questions, which leads to the signature tea and another twenty minutes of nodding and sharing my favorite photographers.

After the second cup of tea, she says she can't wait to see the pictures, that they're going to help me a lot. The clock reads 4:10, forty minutes past dismissal. Ms. K reminds me of our next family meeting.

"Right," I say. "We'll be here."

I stay on the couch for a few more minutes.

"Did you need anything, Miriam?"

"No, no."

"Did you have a question?"

"No."

"You just came in to tell me about your project and how excited you are about it?"

"You really can't wait to see the pictures?" I ask.

She smiles.

"That's pretty much it," I say.

"Do you have a ride home? Is your father picking you up?"

"Nope. He brings me in. You know, for now."

She's looking for her phone, packing her bag, grabbing her coat. She's in a hurry.

"Well then, let's walk out together. I have a workshop this afternoon."

"Oh."

"It's in Columbia Heights, and it's rush hour so I have to run. I would stay if you needed me."

"Of course. No, no, no. I'm fine. I was just checking in."

"All right then."

Ms. K closes the door and says goodbye to everyone in the adjoining offices. Most people have cleared out already, except for the athletes and the extracurriculars. I exit through the parking lot with Ms. K so I won't run into Adam, in case he's still waiting after forty-five minutes. We both squint as we say goodbye. The days are getting shorter; the sun struggles to stay above the roof of the gym.

"You know I can't give you a ride," Ms. K says.

"Right."

"I would, but I can't."

"I don't need a ride. I'll walk. It's nice out."

"They said it might rain tomorrow. That's too bad, right? Not that you trick or treat."

"No, but my mom usually makes me sit with her on the porch until the last candy has been given out."

"That's nice. I'm gonna have to get a poncho for my niece," she says, shielding her eyes from that sun.

Neither one of us wants to be the first to leave, but Ms. K has more practice at this, so she smiles broadly, wishes me a good evening, and unlocks her car. She tucks her skirt under her thighs as she slides into the driver's seat. She has a workshop to go to, a car she can steer in the direction she pleases, a job, and a niece to take pictures of. She still has time to have her own children, whenever she's ready. She's not my mother, but she's an adult. I try to reach for that in my future, but it's too far ahead to get a good grip. She rolls down the window and sticks her hand out to say goodbye, or to warn me she is backing out.

"Ms. K?"

She switches out of reverse and hits the brake, looking for my voice. I walk to her window.

"What's she going to be?" I ask.

Ms. K looks confused. There are at least three paper cups on the floor by the passenger seat.

"Who?"

"Your niece ... tomorrow ... what's she going to be for Halloween?"

Ms. K smiles in relief. "A butterfly."

"Of course," I say, "of course."

"I'll see you on Monday, Miriam."

"Yep."

She drives away, and I check my phone: two missed calls, one text. All from Adam.

Where r u? Are u coming? Where is my camera?

I shut my phone and start walking home. Eva's key must be there. This will take me less than two hours, and that's counting a soggy bagel from the Greek coffee place.

# THIRTY-THREE

did you go back home?

# THIRTY-FOUR

Mom presumably stopped smoking when she got pregnant with me. I've seen her pull out a cigarette occasionally, when Dad is really getting to her, but never ever in the house. She always says the pregnancy was a great excuse to quit. Hence the surprise, when I walk in and she's chain-smoking Lucky Strikes on our living room couch.

The smell belongs to another era, a time before cookbooks and NPR, and Mom looks like she's stepped into the time machine herself. She's lying on the couch in her Barnard sweatshirt, her hair like a newly made nest sitting inside the hood. The pack of poison is on the coffee table, where my mother has spread dozens of pictures. She is looking at a print very closely, holding it up to her eyes, while her other hand holds a glass of something the color of pale wood. Switch the setting and she could be twenty. Something tells me I should not interrupt.

"I can't decide if this one is my favorite," she says without looking up.

"Hi Mom," I say, trying not to breathe in the smoke.

"It's the saddest, for sure. With the sweater on the chair, and the mug."

I walk closer. It's definitely whiskey in the glass.

"What are you looking at?" I say.

Mom puts down the Scotch, sits up and picks another print from the coffee table. She examines both closely, not the least bit distracted by my question.

"It's a close call. You are a master at composition, much better than I ever was. You spend so much time in that darkroom, but you've got your eyes open from the start. I can tell these things, you know. It's my job."

"Are those my pictures?" I ask.

"The dog is perfect in this other one. I don't know how you got him to sit so still. It's like he can smell you, but he can't find you. Great use of foreground. Maybe this one wins."

I stomp over and snatch the photo out of her hand. I've seen it before. This is my stuff. I took this picture.

"Why are you looking at these?" I ask.

Mom goes to light another cigarette and finally looks at me and smiles.

"These are my pictures. They are private."

She inhales and shrugs. "They weren't in your darkroom."

"No. They were in my *bed* room. Since when do you go through my stuff?"

This makes her laugh, but not with the same abandon as in Ms. K's room. This laugh is more evil, more condescending.

"What stuff?" she says when she catches her breath. "You got rid of everything you had up there." She looks at the table. "Except for these…"

"This is none of your business."

"This is entirely my business."

"I don't go in your room and look through your shit."

"Watch your mouth."

"Watch my mouth? You're the one who's, like, the rebel, smoking cigarettes and drinking."

She smiles. "You're funny."

"I'm glad you think so. Give me my pictures back."

"I spent all this time talking to you, never pushing you or asking you questions, avoiding power struggles, trusting you."

I start piling up the night pictures, but they're all over the place. She must have been looking at them for a while before I got here. I find a couple on the armchair, three under the table, one on the end table under the lamp.

"Don't do that," she frets. "They're organized. They're in categories."

"They're mine."

Mom rolls her eyes. "I was trying to find a system, to group them by season, by emotion. I was looking for clues. I haven't had this much fun in a while, playing detective with my own daughter."

"You are acting crazy. You shouldn't have taken these."

"I didn't take them."

I've gathered them all except for the one in her hand. "Yes you did."

"Nope."

"You went into my room and found the pictures."

My eyes feel full and wet, but I'm incapable of crying. She puts the cigarettes down and sighs.

"I didn't take the pictures, Miriam."

"Okay. I get it. *I* did."

"No, I mean I didn't *take* them from you."

"I don't understand."

"Adam came by."

"What?"

"Adam came by looking for you. He seemed really upset."

"What did he say?"

"He wanted to talk to you. He said you weren't answering his calls. I told him that you would be home soon and gave him some water. He was really upset, Miriam. He looked like he was about to cry. I asked him if everything was all right, and he said he wasn't sure. He told me he was worried about you, that he didn't know what to do."

"What did you say?"

"Nothing. I just listened."

"Did you tell him about Ms. K?"

"Yes. I figured he knew already. I thought you were with him when you skipped class."

Of course you did.

"Anyway, he started getting uncomfortable. I think he was trying to protect you, so I didn't want to push it. I told him you'd call when you got home."

I have to sit down.

"Before he left, he asked for his camera. He said he'd left it here. He went up to your room to look for it, but it wasn't there. He wanted to go to your darkroom, but I told him I couldn't let him, that we had an agreement."

Although I'm pissed at my mother in her college sweatshirt, I'm also a little bit proud. She's trying so hard.

"You didn't go in?" I ask.

"No, Miriam, and neither did he. He looked everywhere for his camera. He said he was sure you had taken it. I told him you had your own, and he said you were using that for something else. I asked him what he meant, and that's when he gave me the pictures. He said they were upstairs."

"I *cannot* believe it. I can't believe he did that."

"He was worried, Miriam. We're all worried."

"Did he tell you anything else?"

"He gave me this," she says, and hands me a large envelope with my name on it, my full name. It's Adam's handwriting.

"What is it?" I ask.

"I don't know, Miriam. Believe it or not, I do try to respect your privacy. Open it."

I start to open it and see there's a picture in there. I close it back up.

"Did he say anything else?" I ask.

"Like what?"

"Nothing. Forget it."

"What was he supposed to tell me?" Mom says.

"Nothing. I'm going over to his house."

"I'll take you."

"It's five blocks away."

"It's cold. Let me take you."

"These are my pictures, Mom."

"They're good."

"I don't know, but you weren't supposed to see them."

"You took them in the middle of the night," she says.

"This is why you weren't supposed to see them. I'm *so* mad. I'm so mad."

"I'm taking you to Adam's."

"Mom?"

"Miriam?"

"Fine. But you're waiting in the car."

"Sounds good. Bring his camera."

"We'll see. Haven't you, like, been drinking?"

"Miriam. I'm your mother. I'm the most responsible person you know. I had a sip of whiskey."

She takes the pictures from my hand, straightens the corners in the pile, and lays them in the middle of the coffee table. "Let me get the keys."

When she walks out, I breathe and open the envelope. There she is again, this time in black and white: it's the same picture I saw in his camera. Eva and the sculpture, my two Picassos. One standing, and one lying down, looking at each other for the first time.

# THIRTY-FIVE

It's cold enough to turn the heat on in the car. I know the way to Adam's with my eyes closed. First right, three blocks, speed bump, make a left, semi-circle around the cul-de-sac. I close my eyes to test myself and peek after my mother misses the second turn.

"You're going the wrong way."

She locks the door. "We're not going to Adam's."

"What? Where are we going?"

"We're not going to Adam's until you talk."

"You can't do this."

"Then talk."

"Are you kidnapping me? Talk about what ?"

"Whatever you want. I will drive until you tell me what's going on. Something is going on."

"This is crazy."

"Possibly."

"You can't keep me in here. You can't *make* me talk."

Mom is wearing her glasses now, which makes her look like she's been up all night reading. She used to live in New York, without any money, or car, or children. The city is her most painful ex-boyfriend, her greatest heartbreak, her Elliot. You can tell by the way she dismisses it when people bring up the all-night bodegas, or the energy and the art scene. *The only thing I miss is the subway,* she always says. She had a filthy apartment by the Hudson River. I know because, a few years ago, our family froze its collective ass looking for it. When we finally got there, we all stood on the opposite sidewalk and looked up, following the fire escape stairs to the third floor. The wind was ruthless. Mom cried. Dad pulled her close, and nobody said a word until lunch.

We skipped New York the following year.

I pull the handle on our old Volvo. I have been childlocked. We are in the middle of rush hour, so the ride is an awkward dance of stop and go. Mom knows all the shortcuts and back roads, since she has lived in DC for twenty years now. We inch across a major intersection and dip back into the streets lined with houses, most of them covered in sagging spiderwebs, jack-o'-lanterns, bats, and other scary things.

"Where are we going?" I say.

"I don't know. Where do you want to go?"

"Oh, the illusion of choice."

"Don't get smart with me. I'm actually enjoying this," she says.

"Oh, good. I'm not."

That's not the entire truth. Actually, this is the calmest

I have felt since my bathroom discovery. Something about being driven somewhere by my mother, something about being warm inside this car.

"Can I turn on the music?" I ask.

"I'd rather not. Thanks for asking."

"How about the radio?"

"Same."

We zoom under the Kennedy Center, and I lean my head toward the Potomac.

"It's dark. Won't Dad be worried?"

"You don't seem to mind the dark," she says, "and Dad's already worried."

Mom crosses the bridge to Virginia and we drive on the GW Parkway, where the traffic gives us time to admire the sights across the river. There is nothing as white as the monuments at night. The whole scene is like a giant clay model. We don't have a skyline here in DC. We have a museum.

"It's pretty," I say.

"This is where Dad used to take me when I missed New York too much."

"Do you still miss New York?"

"Rarely. Sometimes I do."

"When Ari comes to visit?"

"When I listen to music."

"Why is that?"

"I fell in love with music in college. When Opa and Oma finally agreed that it was best for me stay on campus, instead of commuting from Jersey, I bought myself a Walkman." She snickers. "Do you even know what that is?"

"Of course I do."

"Well, I got one, to celebrate my independence, you know. We used to trade tapes in the dorms. Nineteen eighty-two was a big year. Madonna had just come out with her first single, Joni Mitchell got married in Malibu. Ozzy Osbourne got arrested for pissing on the Alamo."

"Watch your mouth," I say.

Mom smiles.

"But I was in love with Morrissey," she says.

"I know Morrissey." I beam. "From the Smiths."

"Good girl. That's right."

I wish I could take credit for knowing something about music, but everything remotely interesting has come from my sellout ex-boyfriend.

"Anyway. I had this Smiths tape that one of Ari's punk friends had given her."

Ari is Mom's best college friend. She comes over once every couple of years, and they spend three days eating and drinking and talking. No one is allowed to bother them. If you speak, they don't listen. I can do whatever I want when Ari comes to DC.

"Ari had punk friends?" I say. "She has, like, a million children."

"Five. She has five children. But, yes, she had a lot of friends you wouldn't necessarily imagine her with. She was a bit of a rebel. A disciplined rebel."

We are passing the housing projects right before Old Town. After we cross King Street, Mom turns into the quaint cobblestone streets and we bump around between the dark, tiny houses on the historic register list.

"Their first album had just come out, and only the coolest of the cool knew about it. Ari left it on her desk, and I picked it up one day. Ari was always home on the weekends our first two years. That was before her parents kicked her out of the house."

"What? Why did they do that?"

"I guess I never told you that story. Ari fell in love with a guy at Columbia. Her parents didn't approve."

"She couldn't date?"

The streets are deserted. Everybody is saving for tomorrow, when they'll all turn into wizards and witches and bleeding zombies.

"Oh, she could date. She was supposed to find a husband."

"So what was the issue?"

"The guy was an atheist."

"Like a reform guy?"

"Like not Jewish. Like did not believe in God."

"Oh."

"Right," she says. "Oh."

We drive out of town, back to the Parkway, where the cars in front of us start to disappear into their exits until it's just us, as far as I can see. I check the gas meter. We have a half tank. The lights flood the trees as we pass. We're heading to Mount Vernon, George Washington's place. I bet it's really pretty here during the day.

"So what happened?" I ask.

"They stuck together until senior year. She stopped talking to her parents and most of her extended family ignored her. Her sister would occasionally bring food on Friday, or stop by when she was in the city visiting."

"Where did her family live?"

"Brooklyn."

"Isn't that in the city?"

"It was different in the eighties. Brooklyn was far in the eighties."

"Were they Hasids?"

"Not quite, not the way you picture it. They were committed. They were traditional. They didn't have beards, if that's what you are asking."

I roll my eyes.

"What were they scared of?" I say.

"Of change, of losing something. Of not honoring having lost something."

"What happened with the guy?"

"His name was John. He moved to California. She stayed in New York."

"What happened?"

"Nothing."

"What do you mean, nothing? She gave everything up, after all that trouble?"

"It's not everything. He asked her to go, and she said no, and that was that. That's all she gave up."

We've reached George Washington's estate. The parking lot is closed, but there are still a few tour buses hanging out with their headlights off. Mom goes around the circle and heads back to the street.

"Why did she say no?"

"He wasn't Jewish."

On the way back, she takes a less scenic route, past strip malls and mega churches and *pupuserias*. The day laborers are jumping off pick-up trucks, coated in paint and dirt, and walking home to their crammed apartments, making a call to their wives back in El Salvador.

"Can we stop for some food?" I say.

"Are you hungry?"

"Starving."

"There's some cashews in the glove compartment."

The cashews look withered and smushed in their bag.

"How about Chinese? Isn't there a decent Chinese restaurant out here?"

"This isn't a date, Miriam."

"No. It isn't."

"You want to start talking?"

"About what?"

"Let's start with the pictures. Since when are you taking pictures in the middle of the night?"

Mom moves confidently through the spiderweb of the Metropolitan area, where the cars split toward the South, the North, and the Federal. Georgetown looks like a medieval village on the hill across the river.

"I can't sleep. I couldn't sleep."

"Why not?"

"I don't know. I just *hear* everything."

"Couldn't you tell me about it? I could have helped you. How long has this been going on? Are you going by yourself? How do you even get to these places? You're a girl. It's the middle of the night. You could've been hurt."

"Jesus, Mom. If you want me to talk, maybe you should let me."

"You're right. I'm sorry. Fine. Go on."

"Well, you shouldn't be worried."

"Why not?"

"Because the pictures are nothing. They're just pictures."

"So why is Adam so upset?"

"Because Adam is Adam, and he makes big deals."

"And you don't?"

"I make big deals out of *big* things."

"Adam is the best friend you've ever had. And the smartest. Unlike other people."

I decide against slamming her head into the steering wheel, for now. I remember what she doesn't know, and it helps me feel sorry for her.

"Whatever," I say.

"Not whatever, Miriam. I'm your mother. We came to get you at the train station in the middle of your trip this summer, and now you haven't slept for two months. You're going to tell me what happened, or we're going to run out of gas in West Virginia."

"You're a bully."

"You can't change this."

The thing is, she doesn't have to push me because I have been waiting to say something, anything, to anyone for a while now. I want to talk about the fight, and the sculpture, and Adam. I've just gotten used to being silent; silence has become the place I live in, like a room that gets messier and messier, but gradually, so you think it's actually normal. You think this must be what it always looked like.

"He didn't stand up for me," I say, tentatively.

"Okay ..."

"His dad made a really stupid comment, and he didn't say anything."

She pauses. "What did his father say?"

"It's so embarrassing. I don't even want to repeat it."

"I've probably heard it," she says.

I take a breath. "Something about how art and faith don't save lives. How we should stop investing in things we can't count on."

My eyes start to sting with the same rage and confusion. I watch my mother's face and see no anger, just bones and lines and silence.

"Did *you* say something?"

"Not much. What was I supposed to say?"

"Well, what was *Elliot* supposed to say?"

"Oh my God. You're taking his side."

She rolls her eyes and almost misses a stop sign in front of Georgetown Hospital. This is where I was born. Six weeks early. July 23rd. Barely a lion.

"I'm not taking any sides, Miriam. I'm just trying to figure out what you wanted."

"I can't believe you."

"You can't expect him to feel as strongly as you do about this."

I think back to the sculpture and Eva. How strongly we both felt, how angry. She was right. She would understand. I promise myself to check for her key again as soon as we get back home. I'm going to get her that picture. I'm going to find her.

"I do expect that, Mom."

"Honey..."

"Mom, I pushed the Picasso at the museum. I did it."

The stillness, the creepy hum of the truth, the gratitude my body feels at finally letting go. All of that precedes the look of terror on my mother's face. I see, for the first and last time in this story, that I have robbed her of something I don't even understand. For the next few minutes, she gives me permission to wonder what *she* is thinking, because she can't call the guards fast enough, she can't get her face together in time. That window, that empathy, saves me, in a *Freaky Friday* way, because it makes me look at me.

# THIRTY~SIX

This is how the truth comes out. In traffic, at night, in her Barnard sweatshirt, in a car I can't even drive. She takes one trembling hand off the wheel and looks for mine, and then she holds it tight so the sweat won't let it slip, and I cry. I cry so hard my head hurts for the next three days, so hard I have to blow my nose in the sleeve of my favorite shirt, so hard the lights blur into a mess of white and blue and red and green, and I let them. I don't force my eyes to focus, like I would the camera.

My mother does not say a word. She just squeezes my hand tighter every time I sob, making every effort not to stop me or talk me out of it, knowing that if she opens her mouth, she might run us into the World War II Memorial. We pass the monuments on the Mall, and she finally turns into the parking lot next to the Albert Einstein statue. She lets my hand go, gets out, and waits for me on the sidewalk.

When I peek through the bushes, I see the genius is still smiling. I used to climb on his bronze pants, step on his bronze papers, pet his bronze mustache. When I learned to read, I would trace the letters carved on the granite bench. This is what they say: *The right to search for truth implies also a duty; one must not conceal any part of what one has recognized to be true.*

Perhaps that's right, but truth is a motherfucker sometimes, selective and cruel. We walk to the stoplight and wait for the crossing man to turn green. It's chilly out. The air bites where the tears have dried, on my neck and cheeks. My nose must be enormous. It always swells after I cry. The cold has scared most other people back into their hotels. Tomorrow is Halloween.

I struggle to keep up with my mom, and wonder if I should grab her hand again, or if she wants to be alone, if she even wants me here. We walk under the trees toward a bright yellow light, until we've crossed the concrete barricades and are facing the Lincoln Memorial. There's no moon in the reflecting pool.

We walk all the way up to the top, where Lincoln sits like a wise giant in his temple. My dad would kill us if he knew we came here without him. As my mom reads (or pretends to read) the inaugural address, I lean on a yellow column. I am only a mortal. My mother is neither sad nor pissed. She's lost, and she's looking for strength in a man made of marble. When I've had enough of the tension, I walk down the stairs, letting all my weight fall with every step, hoping it will startle me into something real. You have a dream. I have a dream too, an impossible one.

This moment is beautiful, even if it's scary, even if it's sad. It's our détente. I know it will all be spoiled, that it will be real by sunrise. I will have to look my mother in the face, and she will have to say something uglier than the Gettysburg Address. Her words will not fix anything. It will have to be something about what comes next.

When I get to the bottom of the steps, a couple asks me to take their picture, and I'm too tired to say no. One, two, three and take a picture of their two matching grins. They're having a good time. I have to give Adam his camera. I have to get Bogart back from Eva. I'm going to have to explain everything.

When we get back in the car, my mother turns on the heat and says: "You are telling your father."

I nod and swallow. My angry-girl mask dropped as soon as I told her the news. Someone has to tell him, so I will.

Back in the city (ours, not hers), when we cross the Buffalo Bridge over Rock Creek, I tell her I'm sorry, and she tells me I don't need to apologize; we just need to deal with it. *We.* I let the plural go, since I'm too exhausted to fight. I feel like I've run a hundred marathons but never once crossed the finish line. Like I can't get to the end. It's past nine thirty, and although we're both tired and my mother might appreciate some time to herself, it seems wrong for me to fall asleep right now. Tonight, she will cry when I close my bedroom door. She has not cried yet. My eyes are losing focus.

"Maybe she just didn't want to go to California," I say, super drowsy.

"Who?"

"Ari. Maybe she just didn't want to leave New York."

"Yes," my mother says. "Maybe."

"Or maybe she didn't want to be with him."

"I doubt that."

My mom gives me a sideways glance, her eyes puffy and tired, her hands gripping the wheel to make it home.

"Do you think she's happy?" I ask.

"I think she's fine."

"Fine?"

"Fine. Good. Great. She has a good life, beautiful kids, funny friends, a husband who says yes most of the time."

The leather squeaks under my sinking body.

"You think she should've gone."

"I think she should've been a dancer. She was a wonderful dancer, one of the best I've ever seen."

"You smell terrible, Ma. You shouldn't smoke."

"I know."

When we get home, I'm asleep and it's my father who comes back to the car to wake me up. He can't carry me anymore, but he keeps his hand on my back as we walk to the door. Inside, across the hall, he's strung the prints of the night pictures, with pins, on an old clothesline. It's overwhelming. Sometimes he's so far away and in his head, and then he just comes close, or notices something, or pays attention, and it always overwhelms me.

"Thanks Dad."

"Sure. They're pretty. I don't know when the hell … "

"I just need to go to sleep."

"We'll talk tomorrow?"

"Yes."

"Good night, bean."

"Good night."

I duck under the pictures to go up the stairs. I can hear the shower on in the master bathroom. Eva's key is nowhere to be found. Today was Shabbat and nobody said a word.

# THIRTY~SEVEN

is it your mom?

# THIRTY-EIGHT

It turns out I didn't have to tell him after all. He already knew.

"What do you mean, *you knew it*? Did Mom tell you last night?" I say.

"No. I just knew it. I knew there was a reason you were skipping class."

Maybe it's best if I leave Eva out of this.

"Why?" he says.

"Why what?" I ask.

"Why did you push the sculpture?" my father asks.

"We don't know that she did it on purpose," says my mother, in a rasp that betrays last night's smoking relapse. "Not yet."

My dad sighs. "Well, Sarah, this didn't just happen. It's been a week already and she hasn't told anybody. She's snuck out of the house. Many times. She's been lying. A lot."

He exhales loudly and turns to me again.

"How did the sculpture find the ground, Miriam?"

My mother rolls her eyes.

"What now, Sarah? What did I say now?"

"It's not time to be cute, Seth."

The light is coming in, bright and unforgiving through the kitchen window.

"I know that, Sarah," he snaps. "I'm just trying to finish a sentence here, and you keep interrupting me with your corrections."

"It matters. How we talk about it matters."

"You think I don't know that? I don't have to be her mother to know that. How long have *you* had to come up with the right way to talk about this? A day? Two days? A week? Is this why you went hysterical in that counselor's office?"

This is the first time since I rode in a car seat that I've heard my father raise his voice with my mother. It's usually the other way around, and even that is rare.

"What time is it?" I blurt.

"Miriam ... " my father starts, keeping one hand on the counter to signal he's not done with my mother.

"Aren't you supposed to be going to the market?" I say.

"Nobody's going anywhere," Mom says softly.

She turns to my father.

"She told me last night. And I told her she had to tell you."

"Of course she had to tell me. Were you thinking of not telling me?"

Even this last question seems to be for my mother, as if I am not in the room.

"Seth, I think we should both calm down."

"Were you calm when she told you? Would you like it better if we excused ourselves and had a private talk in the living room about how best to react to the biggest mess in our daughter's life?"

"Hey," my mother objects, like a coach calling a foul. "You think I don't know it's a mess? I'm the one with the art gallery. I'm the one who taught her to take pictures. You don't think I'm hurt?"

"This isn't about you, Sarah," he says.

"We don't know what it's about, Seth."

"Then why don't we ask her, for God's sake."

"It was Elliot," I shout. "I guess *is. Was. Whatever.* Elliot is the reason I pushed the sculpture. Adam is the reason I pushed it. You're the reason I pushed it. All of you. I'm the reason I pushed it, and I'm the one who has to live with that."

Their heads turn to me in tired disbelief. My father's face falls straight into his palms, pushing his glasses away from his head in a clownish gesture, something that would've made me giggle and ask for more only ten years ago. My mom puts her hand on his shoulder and they stand there like that, until his shoulders start to move up and down and she pulls him close to her and they embrace, in our kitchen, right in front of me, in a manner so urgent and intimate I have to get away, and the only place to go is back into my green ocean.

Adam has called me nine times since I left school yesterday, since I silenced my phone to avoid talking to him. He has not left a single message. The last call was early this morning. I dial his number hoping to get his voicemail, and there it is. Thank God for his Saturday runs with his dad. I hang up before the recorded voice. My parents are loading the dishwasher downstairs. I brush my teeth so hard my gums start to bleed.

"Miriam?"

I spit the red water out. "Yes?"

"I brought breakfast."

"I'm not hungry. Thank you."

She opens the door and leaves a tray with a defrosted bagel and tea inside the room. She even peeled and sectioned an orange for me, arranging the half-moons in a circle on a paper towel.

"Thanks, Mom."

"What are you doing?"

"I was just brushing my teeth."

"Hmm."

"Adam called my phone this morning," she says.

"What did he say?"

"I don't know. I didn't pick up."

Sometime between her breakfast and mine, Mom has showered and dressed. Her skin is red in the places where she rubbed in her face cream, and she's wearing her orange Halloween sweater.

"Does he know?"

I shake my head.

"We have to talk about what we're going to do," she says.

"I know, Mom. I know."

"You should think about it."

"I will."

"You had a long night."

"So did you."

She looks exhausted.

"I'm sorry about the fight down there. We're just confused and scared. We're just trying ... " she says.

"It's fine, Mom, I get it."

She breathes and gathers her strength. "I called Ms. K this morning."

"I wish you would have asked me," I say.

"Well, you will have to face this, and I don't know where to start."

"Who else?"

"That's it. Your father and I haven't decided what to do yet."

"Didn't you say we should do it together?"

"I know you know this, but it's a big deal. I know a lot of the people who work there, Miriam. I can't lie to them."

"I get it. I'm in trouble."

"We'll figure it out," she says.

"Okay," I say.

She grabs her braid and pulls at the strands to thicken the end.

"Am I going to school on Monday?"

"Well, you have to go back eventually. Why are you asking that?"

"I don't know. Sorry..."

"Maybe we can all go for a walk somewhere today."

"I don't really feel like going outside. Where's Dad?"

"He went for a run."

My father detests running. He thinks only dumb people run. He thinks there's no reason to run when you can walk or ride a bike. The only reason my dad would be caught running is if someone or something was chasing after him.

"Is he coming back?"

She smirks again, and I'm relieved that I can still make her smile.

"I thought you said nobody's going anywhere. He hates running."

My mother sighs and sits on the very edge of the very corner of my bed, trying not to take up too much room.

"I know it's hard to see him like that, Miriam. You just need to give him a little time. He left because he doesn't want to hurt you."

That seems to be a trend with men. Leaving you so they don't hurt you. Either a trend or a method.

"Does that seem right to you?"

"Everybody has their way."

"I don't understand what that means."

"I don't know if it's right, Miriam. It's what he needs, and I need him to do what he needs to do."

There's a certain level of logic, or absence of logic, that belongs only in a long marriage. More than ten years, at least. It's a whole different set of rules, as if they are all keepers of powerful secrets, and they constantly remind you that they know something you don't know, and then when you're finally interested, they can't explain it. Like they don't have the words to pass it on. So all you get is this vacant look or half-hearted sigh. A glass panel divides your lives, stupid faces on each side.

"I'll call you when he gets back. Or he'll come up to check on you," she says.

"I'm just not sure what we're all supposed to be doing."

She's looking for the words.

"We wanted to be here for you. You have to take responsibility, but we don't want to leave you alone."

"Okay. Thanks."

As they go for runs and make breakfast, I float around in my home like oil in water. The more they crowd me, the more I'm convinced this is really my problem to solve.

My mother sneaks out to do something quiet, maybe fold towels. I stick my finger in the bagel hole, wear it like a ring, and bite around the edges. The tea bag is still in the water and the tea is turning too dark to drink without milk. I take a sip. She forgot to bring up the milk. I don't want to go down there to get it.

I decide against getting dressed, since that may suggest that I am up for the walk. If they ask, I will go, but I don't want to encourage it. I have been spending enough time outside. I dial Eva's number and get her voice mail again. I hang up. I dial the number again and leave a message.

"Hi Eva, it's Miriam. I haven't talked to you since the zoo, which I know you know, but I thought I'd remind you. Anyway, I tried to call you and I sent you a couple of messages, but you haven't called me back. I guess you know that too. So, I don't know if you've gone back home or anything, and if you have that's great—"

*If you are satisfied with your message, please press one. Otherwise, press two for more options.*

Try again. Straight to voicemail, again.

"Hi, it's me again. I got cut off in the middle of my message, so I'll try to make this one short. I don't know where you are, but I'm home. I told my parents about the Picasso. I don't know what's going to happen. I do need my camera. Anyway, give me a call if you want to meet. Bye."

She probably won't call back until I say I got Pablo in a picture. She was pretty clear about that. There's a chance that she just went back. Maybe she is getting out the face paint for this afternoon, or buying candy for her brother. All of those things are far better than a blurry picture. Maybe she's done with me.

"Miriam?" The knock comes a second after the voice. "Adam's here."

"Here?"

My father pops his face in, and I am actually startled by how red it is. The veins on his temples are raised like little green rivers and his shirt has that triangle of sweat only men can produce. He smells like garlic and deodorant.

"Yes. Should I tell him to go?"

I entertain the option. If he tells him to go, Adam will leave, but then I will have to explain why my father showed him out. He might think I told them what happened between us, and that would make him more hopeful than

I can handle right now. That would make it all official. If I tell him to come up, he'll ask me why my father looks like a sweaty eggplant.

"Can you tell him I'm not here?"

"No."

"Why not?"

"Because you are."

"It's quarter to twelve. Shouldn't you be dressed?" I say.

"Are you asking me that right now?"

I walk past my dad to go downstairs and find Adam in the threshold, hands in the pockets of a brown hoodie, cheeks flushed from what looks like a fast walk over. His eyes are foggy and red, but fixed on mine with an intensity that makes me want to sit down.

"Can I come in?"

"Yeah. Hi. We should stay down here. My parents are upstairs."

"Sure. I have half an hour, then I have to get back home to help my parents with something."

He's not interested in why my parents are acting weird. He doesn't even notice. His eyes and hands speak other urgent matters. This is inevitable. This is happening no matter what I do.

"Where were you yesterday? We were supposed to meet at the gate."

"I know. I had a meeting with a teacher."

"And your phone wasn't charged. For the entire afternoon, the whole night. It's probably still out, right?"

"Adam."

"So is your dad's, and your mom's, and I bet your landline is busted too. Along with your computer. And your legs, since I live five blocks from here."

"It's been a rough couple of days."

"Because of Thursday?"

"This has nothing to do with you."

"Bullshit."

"You shouldn't have showed her my pictures."

"Why not? She must've liked them. They're up."

He points to the pictures hung across the entrance hall. I'd forgotten about them. They make me sad. It makes me sad that my dad left them up there, that he had to duck under them on his way out for his run.

"You know that's not the reason why you showed her the pictures."

"Why did I show her the pictures, then?"

"Because you were mad at me."

"Wrong, Miriam Feldman. One hundred percent wrong."

I stop my eyes mid-way to the ceiling.

"I gave her the pictures because I wanted to see you."

There's nothing I can say to this face, not now.

"You want to be a big mystery? All right. Well, then don't act surprised if everybody's looking all over for you. We would all just chill out if you would just tell us."

"Who's *we?* Tell us what?"

"Where's my camera, Meem?"

"Upstairs," I hiss, which makes Adam lower his eyes,

which gives me a little more steam. "You wanted to see me. I'm here. What?"

He straightens up a little, and the bumps on his sweater smooth out. There's a piece of lint in his hair I'm not allowed to pick out. He presses his palms together and looks at me.

"You need to tell me." He starts to crack his fingers, one by one. "I already told you. Now you need to tell me. Because I'm not going to wait for you after school if you don't want to be there. With me. You don't know what that's like. I'm not going to just sit here and come up with stupid tricks to get you to pay attention to me. I'm not sad about what happened. I loved kissing you. So I'm not going to sit here and watch you ruin it for me. If you want me, I'm here. If you don't, that's it. I will get used to it. I will get over it. But you have to tell me."

"You already know," I say.

"Obviously not."

"You know how I feel about you."

"I don't. That's why I'm here. That and my camera."

"Look, I don't want to hurt you."

"You should just go get my camera."

"Adam."

"You still can't answer the question."

"What question?"

"Forget it, Miriam."

"Adam, did you take a key?"

"What are you talking about?"

"Adam?"

"What?"

"I told them it was me. I told them about pushing the sculpture."

His eyes narrow right before they get huge, with something that looks horribly like surprise, and that's when I realize he didn't know. When he said he'd known from the beginning, he wasn't talking about Picasso. He was talking about me.

"You didn't know … " I whisper.

He rubs his eyes and shakes his head.

"Can you say something?" I ask.

"You've changed," he says. "You gave up."

Just like that. The unadulterated truth only your best friend is allowed to tell.

# THIRTY~NINE

you are scaring me and you have my camera.

# FORTY

My parents are sitting on my carpet, surrounded by piles of children's books of all shapes, colors and sizes. There are two cardboard boxes next to the bed. They must've gotten them down from the attic. I recognize some of the books. Others, I can't remember at all. My mother's long hair is loose now, still damp from the shower. My father is wearing his sweat-pants. He balances a book on his crossed legs and she leans forward to look at the pictures. The room is silent except for their quiet smiles and the pages turning.

I have no idea if they heard any of my conversation with Adam, and I feel weak at the thought of having one more secret. I tiptoe past my room into theirs, where the bed is still unmade and the trails of their little worlds are everywhere. My father's change is on the night table, along with a few gum wrappers and the leather case for his glasses. My mom's sweatshirt from last night is on their beat-up yellow armchair, which they bought when they met and have moved to every house since.

I haven't been in this room in ages. I can sleep through the night now. Her clothes are too big for me, her shoes too small, my nightmares impossible to rub away. I have had no reason to come here in years.

I sit in the chair and scan the room for clues. I want to know what the difference is, the real difference between them and me. The car keys are on the old dresser. Her bra is plainer than mine, a little padded, less girly. He is reading three books; one is about Lincoln. Her *New Yorker* magazine is open. Her hand lotion is by the lamp. On the way to their bathroom, a pair of striped boxers on the floor makes me wince, until I remember he uses them to blow his trombone-nose in the morning.

The mirror is still a little foggy. There is only one sink, but an imaginary line divides it. On one side: shaving creams, a real razor, bright green mouthwash and a crusty soap. On the other: tubs of creams with the names of exotic flowers, fancy muds and minerals—a red toothbrush and a green toothbrush, both frayed and slightly yellow. I make room in the mirror for my face, which looks puffy and dry. I stretch the skin to make my eyes droop, and examine the blackheads on my nose. When I pull back my bangs, my forehead looks huge.

I pick a tub and twist the top to find a thick gray paste. *Apply on clear skin with your fingertips in a circular motion.* I splash my face with warm water, wipe it clean, and scoop the clay with my index finger. I paint a line down the bridge of my nose, two across my cheeks, another above my lip, on my chin, under the bangs, until my face is the color of the Dead Sea. Down the hall, they are talking about my old books. I wash the mask off with warm water and walk over. The door is still open.

My mother looks up first.

"We're reading your books," she says.

I smile a tired smile. My face feels tingly and new.

"I can't believe we still have all of these. We found them all in the attic."

"Oh," I say.

Mom closes the book she was reading and keeps a finger on the page to hold her place. "Is everything okay with Adam?" she asks.

I sigh. "Not really."

She pats the carpet next to her and my father scoots to make room between them. There is something about warmth that makes us all weak, and something about mothers. If I touch her, or if I let her touch me, that warmth will trick me into feeling safe, and I will talk. And if I talk, I might say what I actually mean. And if I say what I mean, I will know what that is, but I will not know how to forget it. She leaves her hand on the floor to reserve my spot, and my father waits patiently right next to her.

"I lost everything," I say. "It's my fault."

My father looks away, toward Mr. Wallace's ghost. My mom takes a deep breath. Afraid to fall, I sneak in between them and rest my head on her lap, tuck my feet under his knees, and let my hair fall all over my face. Everybody cries in the green room, sometimes silently, sometimes snotty; we cry and cry until my father grabs my toes, shakes them awake, clears his sore throat twice, and opens Rudyard Kipling: "'*The weather door of the smoking room had been left open to the North Atlantic fog, as the big liner rolled and lifted, whistling to warn the fishing-fleet…*'"

And on and on, they take turns reading *Captains Courageous* out loud, and laughing and remembering and sniffing and stopping to catch their breath, then choosing another book and reading once more. We do this for hours, and I lean into the sound of my parents and the rain. I'm almost sleepy when the doorbell rings and interrupts my narrators, and my father gets up to check.

"Trick or treat," a pair of little voices cry.

"Oh my God!" my mother says. "We forgot!"

And as she pats my head, I close my eyes and see a butterfly, under a soaking yellow poncho, holding out her hand, hoping for the best in the bag.

# FORTY~ONE

i told my parents about the picasso. my best friend
hates me. i have nothing to hide. i just want to
know if you are okay.

# FORTY~TWO

It is positively the Day of the Dead at school. The parking lot is basically empty, and it's quiet out here, creepy quiet. Nobody's here except for the music kids; they get to use the recording studio on Sunday. There's a good chance he'll be here. Normally, on the first of November, we'd go out and have burritos, or my mom would stir some cinnamon in hot chocolate and call it Mexican, but this is no longer normally.

Last Halloween, I was Frida Kahlo and Elliot was Diego Rivera. He drew my unibrow with eyeliner, and I pinned thick braids around my head. My mom let me borrow her flashiest shawls, embroidered with blue hummingbirds and thorny roses. I looked more like a lunatic fortune-teller than a self-possessed artist, but I embraced the role and wore my only long skirt. It was freezing. Elliot stuffed pillows under his shirt and brought me a calla lily.

*All you have to do is be fat.*

*Sure, I'll be fat.*

*He was a Marxist.*

*I can be a Marxist.*

We walked around the neighborhood and I took pictures of the decorations while he hobbled around speaking high school Spanish.

"Wasn't Frida a painter?" Elliot said, trying to get me to put the camera away.

"Yes, well, I'm a modern Frida."

"Wouldn't she have hated the camera?"

"Actually, since you are asking, and I'm taking you seriously, Frida's first work was on photographs, or lithographs. Her father used to let her draw on the prints."

"I didn't know that," he said, tracing my brow with his thumb. "And thanks for taking me seriously. How about a treat, comrade?"

I was a little embarrassed to actually ask people for candy, but Elliot tugged my skirt and we walked up to a house with a giant spider. A lady with a pointy hat opened the door, one hand on her hip, the other holding a glass of white wine.

"Señora," Elliot said with a straight face, as confident but much more handsome than his alias, "this is my lovely and talented wife, Frida Kahlo, and I'm her irresponsible husband, Diego Rivera. Trick or treat."

The woman smirked and gave me a Twizzler and Elliot a Snickers, and I felt a little jealous, not of the candy, which may or may not have been a conscious choice, but of the look on her face. I felt alarmed, as if she could take my fat painter away, into her upholstered living room, as if she were a real witch. I even forgot to smile about Elliot's little speech. This was when I knew. If you look back, you can always find the moment when you knew. We just tend to ignore it. House after house, Diego called me Frida, and house after house, they were charmed by his wit and dug out the best candies for him, especially the women. We waited until we were home, then dumped our loot on my mother's shawl and began to sort and eat. On my porch, in between candies, Elliot patted his pillow gut, and I picked dead leaves off my skirt.

"You know what?" he said.

"What?" I said, breaking a Twix so we could share it.

"Frida Kahlo was pretty amazing."

"Indeed," I said, smiling.

"She went through some serious stuff."

I raised my eyebrow.

"I'm serious. I love the painting where she's on the chair and she cuts all her hair off."

"Me too," I said, surprised that my music boy was up on the visual arts. "That's one of my favorites."

"I knew it. You're kind of like her, you know? Without the unibrow, or the parrot, or the fucked-up husband."

"Wow, you really did your research."

"*Claro.*"

I smiled and raked through the bag, looking for Nerds to make my tongue purple, anything to shut out the curious and vain Miriam, the Miriam who wanted to probe about why she was like Frida.

"Is it the mustache?" I asked.

"Nope," Elliot said, "not the mustache."

"She was a much better artist than I am," I said.

"It's not the art either. It's the strength. You know? How you look everything right in the face, how you notice every little thing. I mean, she had a rough life, and I hope you never have that, but you know. I'm just saying—you've got that fire thing, you've got that fight."

I smiled and punched his arm, gently.

"I sound like a loser right now, right? I sound like a loser."

"A fat loser," I said.

We kissed and kissed and bumped fake belly and shawl, mixed real sugar and fake.

That was last Halloween. Frida would kick me in the shins if she could see me right now, and Diego would not be driving the car that I'm trying hard not to lean on. I don't have a right to anymore. He's not my boyfriend. He's not even my fucking friend.

I pray to the Name (who may or may not be willing to listen, at this point) that Elliot doesn't walk out with Maggie. He gives me a break on that, and he slows down when he sees me, but he doesn't exactly stop. He's wearing one of those old-lady cardigans that hipsters make use of. It's wool and dark green, and at least one button is missing. His hands are hidden in the pockets, stretching it over his hips.

"Hi," he says.

"Hi."

"How are you doing?" he says, looking slightly guilty.

"Okay. How are you?"

"Good, pretty good. I haven't seen you since the Smithsonian trip."

"Yeah. I've been here, just a lot of work, you know. "

"Yeah, it's sort of killing me, this whole college thing. I'm sure you've got it figured out. I'm sure the Green is, like, *shoving* you to art school."

My heart warms at hearing Elliot use our old nickname, but my brain knows this is not going to be an easy conversation, and the underhanded flattery only makes it worse.

"Yeah, not exactly."

Elliot nods with his chin, then does that thing when you puff your cheeks one at a time, like you are waiting for something—the ultimate awkward. We used to finish each other's sentences or never even have time to start one. I must channel my Frida, get to the damn point.

"So, I have to talk to you. That's why I came here."

He looks around. "Sure. Uhm, now? I have a few minutes, but then I have to be somewhere in, like, half an hour."

"Yeah, well, now is better. Actually, now is pretty much it."

"Okay." He sits on the curb and drops his messenger bag. I stay standing. I start counting in my head. I tell myself that if I don't say it when I get to five, everybody I love will die. It worked when I was little and I had to make myself jump into freezing water, or get in the roller coaster line. I take out the Neruda book from my bag, open to "The Song of Despair," and clear my throat. One, two, three, four, five. *"'The memory of you emerges from the night around me...'"*

I cannot look up until I'm done. I cannot look up until I'm done.

*"' ...and in it my longing fell, in you everything sank!'"*

Until I'm done, and I see his face frozen in complete embarrassment. Elliot's mouth is open in a perfect O, like the ghosts from last night. I force myself not to regret this.

"Did you write that?" he says.

I think of Eva and what she would say. How she would laugh in his face. I miss her, and I'm worried about her.

"I didn't. Pablo Neruda did."

"It's good. It's sad."

This was a bad idea.

"I don't know what to say, Miriam."

"It's better in Spanish," I say.

"Are you all right?" he says.

"I'm fine."

"I didn't want to ... " he starts.

"Really. Don't say anything."

He puts his face in his hands and rubs it a hundred times before looking back up at me.

"I'm really sorry. I'm sorry. Shit. I don't know what to say."

I have a terrible urge to take his hand, but I don't.

"Can I lean on your car?" I ask.

He looks surprised. "Yeah. Of course. Are you sure you're okay?"

"I'm all right. Look. I'm not asking for anything. I just needed to do that. I'm not going to bother you anymore."

He looks up at me again, and that ratty sweater makes him look so skinny and weak I almost feel sorry for him.

"You're not bothering me."

"Good. And I also wanted to say that someone gave me this book when I was in trouble, and it helped me understand some stuff."

"I'm glad," he says, waiting for his cue.

"Me too," I say, and there is an awkward minute of silence and fidgeting, where two magnets have forgotten how to be in the same place at the same time.

"I'm glad you're doing okay," he says.

I shrug.

"Thanks for the poem," he says.

"Sure," I say.

"You're brave, Miriam."

"Or stupid," I say.

"Never stupid," he says.

And that's the best I'm going to get, so I consider giving him the book, because that would be a good way to close the scene, and if I were in a movie, that's what I would do, but then I remember Eva and her mother and her Pablo and how she said everything changes, and I think maybe I want to give him the book because I want him to read it and think of me, and that's when I ask myself why I should have to lose him and he should not have to lose me. Why?

So I keep the book, and instead hold out my hand, which he shakes without looking up, and I turn around and leave.

I leave, knowing these things are gradual and I won't feel better right away, but I have to remember I'm already different. I'm already gone.

# FORTY-THREE

The Mall is quiet for a Sunday, and I can hear my boots shuffling against the wet gravel. The sound comforts me. I drag my feet a little, so they'll keep me company. The carousel is done for the day. It's getting dark, and I walk over to the sculpture garden holding my cell phone. The security guard barely fits in her glass hut, and she seems to be busy reading.

i am here.

I don't care if she doesn't know what I mean. Maybe that will make her write me back. She has my Bogart. My knuckles sting. It's November. It's windy and cold. Winter is coming. The steps to the sculpture garden are still shiny from yesterday's rain. The first sculpture is a little man on a horse. They are both leaning back, as if I startled them still. The man has no eyes, just a nose, and the horse is screaming, but I can't hear him. I used to like horses. I used to go to the Rock Creek Park stables with my dad on weekends, and he'd pick me up, so I could reach their faces, and we'd touch the spot between their huge nostrils and feel how soft. *Miriam, gentle...* We laughed when they farted and flinched, and when they swatted a fly with their tail.

After the horse, I make a right and, although my mind can remember the rage, my body stays put. It's busy with other things. I miss the girl who was mad about her boyfriend leaving her behind and wandering the streets at night, looking for a house with the light on. From where I stand now, it looks like all she had to do was be sad until she wasn't anymore. I look up at the surrounding walls and imagine where Eva would have been sitting that day, with her bag, her gold fish, and her black hair.

I recognize the other sculptures, but mine is nowhere to be found. No bronze woman, no plaque with the name and artist and the date of his birth and death. Even the pedestal is gone. Nobody's left a note saying they have taken it away and whether it will ever be back. There is no trace of the thing I pushed over. It seems unfair for the people who come specifically to visit her, who expect to see her. It seems unprofessional for the museum to leave us in the dark.

they took it away.

I thumb the letters into my phone.

Picasso's gone.

Send. No reply. I take a picture of the empty spot.

I start to run toward the Metro. I don't know why I'm running. Maybe because I'm tired of waiting. Maybe because all that open space is making me panic. The phone loses service halfway down the escalator to the Metro and, by the time I get to the platform, it's too late to call Mom and let her know I'll be late for dinner. This shouldn't take too long. The red line is mobbed at Metro Center; I have to guess where the doors will open so I can wait in the right spot. I pick a cluster of ladies in suits. They smell like birthday cake.

A few clusters over, there's a group of loud dickheads pretending to push each other onto the rails. Most people ignore them, or quietly shake their heads, until this old guy with a suitcase on wheels just yells "Hey" and they stop and shut up for a second. But as soon as they locate the yeller, they burst out laughing and take turns yelling "Hey." I feel sorry for the guy, probably because he reminds me of my dad. I try to make eye contact with him, so he knows we aren't all little shits.

While I'm getting pushed around in the car, I get really scared someone is going to steal my phone, because I need my phone in case she calls, so I take it out and hold it, but my hands are sweating like crazy. At every stop the car leaks a few people, but there are still no seats left and I am starting to feel the panic. I breathe deep and try singing something in my head to distract me. All I need is a little air. I get off at the next stop, so I can sit down and breathe. I'm still pretty far from home, and I don't know this area well. The elevator is broken and it takes forever to surface.

I find a bus bench and the cold air feels good on my face.

It's been exactly nine days since this all started. Everybody hurries home. The stores are lit and still open, the phones all hot from making weekend plans. Maybe Eva forgot her phone somewhere, or someone stole it on the Metro. Even better, she went back home and got tired of me calling her, so she changed her number altogether. I press the green button, and it goes to her voicemail. I hang up and write the last text:

I need you.

Then I go buy myself a pack of gum.

Chewing three at a time, I walk north toward a cab because I want to sleep tonight, and Eva is standing in the way. She's my last secret. It takes about half an hour, but that gives my stomach time to settle and all that's left is a steady pounding in my head. I spit out the gum, punch out two new ones, and pop them in my mouth before I get out of the car.

The lights are off, and the driveway is empty. Adam's camera is still in my bag. The plan was to take it over after Elliot and apologize. It was a bad plan. I sit down on Eva's front steps and think of the scenarios, of how this could all play out. A few cars roll by, a few heads nod in my direction, but no one who seems to belong in this house.

My phone lights up. One new text message. It's from Eva.

I AM STARTING OVER.

I dial the number but it goes straight to voicemail again. I text back immediately.

Where are you?

Phone lights up.

WITH MY MOM.

Are you okay?

I DON'T KNOW.

I have no idea what to do, so I call my mom, but when she answers and says she's on her way home, it seems impossible to tell her everything. I tell her I'll be later than I thought. She asks me where I am, and I tell her I'm at Elliot's, which is not exactly a lie. It works. She'll wait. I stay at Eva's house, on Eva's doorstep, and wait for someone to come home.

After a few minutes, an SUV slows down and pulls up toward the curb. I can't see who is in there. The driver steps out.

"*Un segundo*," he says before he shuts the door.

My ass is stuck to his steps.

"Hello," he says. I can hear a little accent.

"Hi."

"Are you looking for someone?"

"Uhm, sort of."

Stupid, stupid, stupid. The man is confused, but he doesn't seem mad. He seems nice. He must be the uncle. She never talked about a father. He notices the phone in my hand.

"Are you all right?" he asks.

"Yes." I sigh. "No. Look, I'm really sorry. I'm just ... I know your niece."

His eyes get real big, and he puts his hand on his mouth, and then he looks back at the car. It feels so good to share it with someone that I just want to keep going. No mercy.

"I met her a week ago."

Uncle Eva shakes his head.

"I'm sorry to just show up at your house like this, but I'm sort of looking for her. She borrowed something from me."

"Do you know where she is?" he asks, frantic.

"I'm not sure. Isn't she here?" I say.

"No. Eva hasn't been home in more than a week."

"But I just spoke to her. She said she was with her mom."

His eyes get watery. "*Dios mio*," he says.

He bites his thumbnail and then looks at me like I am a child he should remember to protect.

"What's your name?" he asks.

"Miriam."

"You really know Eva?"

"Yes, sort of, yes."

"How do you know where we live?"

"Because she told me."

"What else do you know?"

"I know her mother is sick, and that she has a little brother. She was really worried about her little brother."

The man's eyes start to water and he bites his knuckle to make himself stop.

"What?" I beg.

"Miriam, I have to talk to my wife. We have to find Eva."

"Have you called her?"

"She does not answer. We thought she was at her boy-friend's house."

"She has a boyfriend?"

"He is a stupid guy, a mean guy, but sometimes she went back. He is the father."

"Whose father?" I ask, but within two seconds, the look on the uncle's face shuts me up. Pablo is not Eva's brother. I look over at the car, where a boy is sitting quietly in his car seat.

"Is that Pablo?"

"Yes," he says.

"And where is Eva's mother?" I ask.

The man shakes his head. "*Se mató*," he says.

"I'm sorry. I don't understand..."

"She's dead, *hija*. My sister, her mother, killed herself."

My head is reeling from too much truth, all at once, and so much pain. I think of the way Eva begged for a picture of her son, of how guilty she felt, how she spoke of her mother. Was she giving me clues? Everything is mixed together: the book of poems, the greasy hair, the gold fish, the altar. I think of the woman in the silver frame, surrounded by candles, and how Eva refused to look at that photograph. She was trying to tell me something, goddam-nit, and I was not listening.

The car window opens and a little head leans over and yells, "Tiiiiiiioooooo. Can we go inside? *Tengo hambre*."

"*Ya voy, mi amor. Un rato, por favor.*"

"So that's Pablo..." I say.

"Yeah, that's Pablo," he says.

"We have to call the police," I say.

He motions for Pablo to wait, and Pablo huffs and grabs a bag of little plastic dinosaurs from the seat pocket. I am sure Eva put those there for him.

"I know what to do," I say.

I got Pablo. He is okay.

Eva's uncle talks to his wife on the phone. He looks lost. I pray for Eva to write back. I promise God everything if he does me this one more favor. The thought crosses my mind that maybe I'm being punished, maybe this is my punishment for pushing the sculpture, for having sex without a condom, for lying to my parents. I beg him for a different punishment, one that does not hurt Eva, Pablo, and this man standing in front of me.

"My wife says we cannot go to the police, because maybe they take away Pablo."

"They would not do that."

"My wife says we need to find her," he says.

I look at Pablo in the car and think of places where his mom might be. His hair is black like hers, but more curly, all over the place. He smiles, and I smile back.

*With my mom*, she said. To find Eva, we have to solve the ultimate puzzle—where the fuck do people go when they die?

"When did you see Eva?" he says.

"The last time was at the zoo," I tell him.

"How many times? Where else?"

"At the park, at my school, at the Cathedral."

He presses his temples to think.

"She was bad?" he asks.

"Bad?" I say.

"Not bad. Sad? She was sad?"

I don't know how to answer. She was everything. She was sad, she was angry, she was funny, she was smart, she was worried, but she did not seem done. I don't believe that. She was the one who helped me. She was hopeful.

"She had hope," I say, wishing that didn't sound so vague and unhelpful.

The man, who looks older by the minute, sighs. "How did you know her?" he asks.

"She found me," I say. "We met at a museum last Friday."

"Last Friday?" he says. "Are you sure it was last Friday?"

"Yes. Why?"

"That's when she left," he says. "She said she needed to get out for a little bit, and my wife took care of Pablo, but Eva did not come back."

He starts shaking his head again, and I'm afraid he's going to cry and I won't know how to comfort him. It strikes me I don't know so much about his niece after all, not as much as he does at least, not as much as his wife does. I see how this was a dangerous game we were playing, how there were parents and children and mourning aunts and uncles involved.

"I'm so sorry to ask you this, but was her mother buried?"

"No. She was burned," he says, a reminder that English is not his first language, that Spanish is, as Eva said to me once, stronger.

I take out the only thing I have that belongs to Eva—the Neruda book—and look for clues as to where she might be. Someone has underlined some phrases or words and there is the occasional comment or star in the margins. All of the scribbling is on the Spanish side of the page. I had assumed that was Eva. I hand the book over to Eva's uncle, hoping he will be able to decipher it better than I can.

"This was Eva's," I say. "She gave it to me when I met her."

He takes the book and looks through it, then turns to the first page and smiles the saddest smile I have ever seen.

"*Por mi hija, la grande poeta de mi vida, para que no tenga miedo,*" he reads.

I wait.

"Her mother gave her this book before … "

I don't wait for him to finish the sentence. It's too horrible. Before she died, Eva's mother left her a book of poems. But poems can't save your life, can they? People do. We have to find her.

"She said her mother liked to take her to the Cathedral. Is that true?" I ask.

Her uncle shrugs. "I don't know. I have never been there."

I try Eva's phone, but it's going straight to voicemail again. She's probably turned it off.

"We have to try every place, one at a time," I say.

"Do you know where to go?" he asks.

"No, but we can try."

The uncle opens the passenger door, and I look back at Pablo, who waves his hand and asks for a goldfish. The irony. The uncle points to a bag and Pablo holds out his palm, where I drop a fistful of orange crackers.

"Thank you," the little guy says.

"You're welcome," I say, and I'm so relieved I finally got him. I have Pablo, Eva. You stay put.

We snake through the cars in rush hour traffic and make our way north, and the uncle and I only talk when he needs directions. He doesn't even tell me his name. When we arrive at the top of the hill, we find a side street to park on and he asks me to wait inside. I want to go, but I understand now that this is not just my story, so I agree to stay in the car and watch Pablo, who seems to be okay with me so long as the goldfish don't run out. I explain to the uncle how to get into the Cathedral, and he takes the car keys, probably because he doesn't want me to run off with the other child in his care. He tells me he'll be right back.

Pablo and I stare at each other for a long minute, then he asks for more goldfish, but instead of eating them, he starts counting.

"One, two, three, four, five," he says.

I notice he's skipped a few crackers, but I'm not sure if I'm supposed to correct him. He doesn't seem to be interested in eating them.

"Actually," I say, "you missed some. Try again."

"Okay—one, two, three, four, five," he says, again skipping two.

I reach for his palm to start counting out loud, but Pablo pops exactly two fish in his mouth before I can get to three. It cracks me up.

"Five!" he says.

He's right. It reminds me of his mom.

"I'm cold," he says.

"Me too," I tell him. "Your uncle will be back soon." I point to the spires of the church.

No word from Eva. I don't know what I was thinking, why I imagined she would update me. I brought him here, I remind myself. That's all that matters.

"Where did he go?" Pablo asks.

I pretend I didn't hear the question, and Pablo messes with the Velcro on his shoes. Except for the Velcro, little boy shoes look like old man shoes.

"Did he go to hear the music?" he asks.

"No," I say.

A few cars roll by, but no one comes out to tell me what to say. He starts squirming in his seat and asks if he can have his ball. I look everywhere for it.

"It's red," he says.

I keep looking, but I can't find it. I tell him I'm sorry and offer more goldfish, but he shakes his head.

"Did you go trick or treating last night?" I ask.

"Yeah," he says.

"It was raining, right?"

"Yeah, but I was a dragon, and dragons can spit fire."

I nod, trying to guess if Eva bought the costume before she left. My heart breaks at the thought of the uncle going to get a polyester dragon at the store.

"But the rain did not kill the fire that I spit, because the rain is little and the fire is big."

"That's right," I say, thinking that *kill* sounds strange coming from a little guy, but I believe him. I believe his dragon.

"My *tío* said I could have four candies because I am four years old, but I had one chocolate one because I am more than three, because my birthday party was in June."

In June, I was in love. I could have had seventeen candies yesterday, and I didn't even have one. June. Was June the date on Eva's neck?

"Were you a princess or a fairy?" he asks.

That makes me laugh a little, and I remember Pablo's thing for dinosaurs.

"I was a dinosaur," I say.

He gives me a serious look, followed by a quick smile, and then he's back to his shoes.

"What dinosaur?" he says.

I can't remember any of the names. It's too long ago.

"The mean one with horns," I say.

"Big?" he asks.

"Huge," I say.

"Triceratops!" He beams, and looks through his bag to hand me a plastic version.

"Exactly!" I say. "Where does a triceratops live?"

Pablo is confused. "I don't know."

"Yeah, that's sort of a stupid question."

"Don't say *stupid*."

I apologize.

"You can say *silly*. We don't say stupid in this house, and my mama says it hurts people."

I tell him he's right.

I don't tell him his mama is missing, and I definitely don't tell him she will be here soon to congratulate him on his impeccable manners because, frankly, I have no idea whether she will or not, and it would be silly for me to give him false hopes. (Is hope what he misses or what he wishes for next? Is hope to smell her neck at bedtime, to count the loops around her jeans, to push his arms through his dinosaur shirt and catch her distracted eyes in front of his? Does he know what to call it when you have something and you can't keep it and then you don't have it and it's with you, all the time?) It's been over a week since he's heard her voice. Only twenty minutes in this car.

He starts to kick his legs like a possessed pair of scissors, and whine. I look for his ball again, but he's getting frustrated. Pablo wants to get out of the car.

"I know, Pablo, but we have to stay here so your uncle can find us when he gets back. He might get worried if we leave. You understand? Does that make sense?"

He doesn't answer, but instead gets quiet and sad-looking. Shit. I made a mistake.

"Hey, you know what?" I say.

Silence.

"Look what I have."

"What?" Pablo says, humoring me.

I pull Adam's camera out of my bag. He was so mad yesterday that he forgot what he came for.

"It's a camera."

I turn it on, switch to automatic, and look through the

viewfinder. There he is, right in front of me. If I move back enough, I can get all his hair. Here he is, Eva, your child, the live, three-dimensional version.

"Can I see it?" he asks.

"You have to be very careful, okay?"

"Why?" he asks.

"Because there are lots of buttons, and it can break if you drop it. It's not mine."

"Is it your mommy's?" he says.

Oh man. My mommy is home, making dinner.

"No. It's my friend's."

"Oh. I'm not gonna drop it," he reassures me.

"Good."

"Because your friend will be very mad if I drop it."

I laugh.

"He probably wouldn't get too mad. He's nice," I say, thinking that's the truth. Even if he said something horrible, that friend is the nicest one I've got.

Pablo holds his little hand out to take the camera. I unbuckle my seat belt and put the strap around his neck. The camera covers most of his face, and, when I tell him to look through the hole, he keeps both eyes open. It's hard for him to keep the thing still.

"You have to look with one eye if you want to see better. You have to close one of your eyes … like a pirate."

Pablo squints. I put one hand over his eye.

"Your hand is cold," he says.

I rub my hands together, against my jeans, and then together again. I put my hand back on his eye.

"How's that?" I say.

Silence.

"What do you see?" I ask.

He puts the camera down. "The car."

I try to remember how my mother taught me. It's too long ago.

"You have to keep looking through the hole, until the picture is done. Or it will come out blurry."

"What's blurry?" he asks.

"Like, fuzzy."

"Like a bear?"

"Like a ... "

"Like a dog?"

"Like the shower door," I say, which is not fuzzy at all.

"I don't like showers."

"Okay. That's okay. Forget that. Let's try again. Keep the camera in front of your face, like this."

I hold the camera and cover his eye with my palm. He lets me.

"Now tell me what you see, on the other side."

"The car."

"Okay. What else?"

"The wheel."

"Great. Now move the camera and keep looking."

I take my hand off Pablo's face.

"Keep looking, don't put the camera down. What do you see?"

"The seat."

"Can you see me through the camera?"

He turns to face me. He moves back, without dropping the camera.

"Yes."

"What do I look like?"

"You have a finger and eyes and a nose. This is heavy."

I reach for the camera, but Pablo plops it on his lap.

"Do you want to take a picture?" I ask.

"I took a picture," he says.

Now I remember. "You *saw* a picture, Pablo. Now you have to take it."

"Okay."

"You look, and move it around, and when you see something you want to keep, you push this button."

It sounds a little loaded for a four-year-old but that's what my mother always told me.

"But you have to be very, very still. You can't move when you push the button."

Pablo brings the camera back up, and I leave his eyes alone. He turns back and forth a little and then points the camera at the church. When he's done, he gives me the camera, and I show him his picture, happily breaking my rule. He smiles and asks if he can take one more. I put the strap back on and he points it straight at me and waits the longest second. *What do you see?* I want to ask, *What do you see?* He pushes the button and tells me he has to pee.

Shit. I don't want to leave the car unlocked, but it's been long enough, and there must be bathrooms somewhere in there. Pablo holds my hand to cross the street and does not let go until we are next to the church, when he breaks free and runs to the side doors. He seems to know the way. I run after him and ask him to stay close. He looks embarrassed. I ask a purple-robed lady where the bathroom is. No sign of Eva or uncle. I would check my phone, but I have no idea what to do if Pablo pees his pants.

I opt for the girl's bathroom. I ask him if he needs help, but he says he can do it by himself and can I wait for him, please. Sure. Pablo comes out of the stall with his shirt half tucked, but I don't say anything, and he tries to jump for the soap, but he can't reach it. I lift him up and run his hands under the water, and we smile at ourselves in the mirror. "Can we go get my *tío* now?" he says as we walk out.

"Okay," I say, hoping I won't disappoint him. "Do you know where to go?"

"Yes," Pablo says, and he laughs, and I feel a hundred times better.

We walk through the large wooden doors, back full-circle into the maze of stained glass and marbles. Pablo grabs my hand. There are flowers in the nave and along the aisles, which could mean a wedding. Pablo launches into a bouquet, inhales, and tells me it's yummy, and we move to the back of the church, toward the tip of the cross. After a few steps, Pablo lets go of my hand and runs full-speed away from me. A few people turn around and I walk faster, until I see who he's heading for.

Eva stands up in a pew next to her uncle. She's wearing my green sweater. Pablo stops before he gets to them and just stands there, frozen. I walk up and stand next to him and he grabs my jacket and tells me that's his mama. I grab Pablo's hand and it's sweaty and warm, and I know it's wrong, but I don't want to let go, so we stay exactly where we are, Pablo's face fixed on his mother.

She walks toward us, and he lets go and walks away from me, and she hurries up and grabs him and hugs him hard, and, although I'm sure he loves her, he doesn't hug her right back, probably because he doesn't know what is in her head.

Pablo asks for a couple of bucks to turn on a candle, and they each light one and say a prayer, which makes me think of my mother, and how she's still here.

# FORTY~FOUR

In the car on the way home, Eva sits in the back with Pablo and he falls asleep on her shoulder. We don't say a word to each other, even though I want to tell her I know everything, especially about her mother, but maybe it doesn't matter now that she's going back. Maybe this is really the end of her trouble. Uncle is driving with one hand, and every once in a while he sighs, like he's letting the air out a little at a time, and I can see in the rearview mirror that Eva's got one hand on Pablo's knee, and they both have their eyes closed now. It would make a great picture.

When we get to my house, the uncle walks over to my side and opens my door, then he shakes my hand really hard and says thank you, about five times. I tell him I'm sorry about all the confusion, and he waves it all away, now that his sister's child is back in his car, now that he can keep his promise. Eva steps out.

"So this is where you live?" she says.

"Yeah," I say.

"It's nice," she says.

"Yeah," I say.

"Look…" she says, and I should stop her, but I don't because I don't want to say goodbye.

"There's a lot going on, but I'm sure you'll be okay," she says.

"Yeah," I say. "You too."

"You have the book?" she asks.

"Uh, actually, your uncle has it, but you should keep it."

"Maybe I can give it to you the next time," she offers.

"Yeah, maybe."

"So what are you going to do about the sculpture?" she says.

"Well, I told my parents, so we have to think of something."

"What are they going to do?"

"I don't know, but they're going to make me tell the truth. They're big on that," I say.

"That's good," she says. "That's hard, but it's good."

"Yeah."

"So…" She looks back at the car. "He's awesome, right?"

And I say, "Your uncle?" which makes her laugh until I say yes, he's awesome, like his mama, and we both look down.

I can't wait any longer, and neither can Eva, so we hug, and she smells like ten days outside your home, sleeping God-knows-where, having God-knows-what nightmares, battling God-knows-what creatures with sharp teeth who

293

eat your hopes for breakfast, lunch, and dinner. She pats my back, and I grab my sweater and whisper that I'm sorry about her mom, because I am, because I can't even imagine. She says thank you again, and it's time to go.

But as she walks away, I see the date, those swirls of ink on her neck, and think it could be either—a birth or a death.

# FORTY-FIVE

Every house on my block has at least one light on. Upstairs or downstairs, people are wrapping up their day, stretching on their couches, checking the movie times, not doing the dishes yet. Most jack-o'-lanterns are still out, and the fake cotton webs are all sagging from last night's rain. My chest won't decide whether it feels light or heavy, but either way, I feel like something is pulling me home. I look back at the street, but their car is gone. Our mailbox is open, and when I reach inside, I find Eva's key. She didn't give me my camera either. It's too late to go after her, and I don't want to bother everybody right now. She knows where I am. I slip the key back in my pocket and make a mental note to put it somewhere safe when I get upstairs. I stop at the door and peek through my window before going in.

The Shabbat candles are lit on the dining room table and Mom, Dad, and Adam are sitting around a pile of pizza delivery boxes. Friday's come and gone, but the special olive plate is out and covered in plastic hot sauce containers. There's an extra place setting, for me. Their faces look softer in the light; Adam's napkin across his lap, Mom's rings, Dad's plate still clean. I blink my eyes like a lens, because I know everything changes. When my mother answers the door, I collapse in her arms, babbling between sobs that I'm sorry I'm late, that I should have lit the candles last Friday. My father and my friend wait patiently behind us, and Adam suggests maybe he should go home, but I tell him he doesn't have to, that I'm sorry about him too. My father tells us all to settle down and stop being sorry and eat some Shabbat pizza instead, and so we do, talking and laughing and ripping our hair out about how the hell does a sculpture just fall when you push it.

# EPILOGUE

*To: Kathryn Lowell, Associate Curator,*
*Hirshhorn Museum*

*From: Miriam Ariel Feldman*

*Dear Señor Picasso,*

*My name is Miriam Feldman, and I pushed your sculpture at the Hirshhorn. Perhaps you are wondering why anybody would do such a thing, but I think you of all people can understand, given that you married twice, had many mistresses, drove everybody crazy, and, in every portrait of you I have ever seen, you look like you never blink. As far as I can tell, you spent your life pushing things. Still, as my mother would say, that doesn't mean that's what I should be doing, and your sculpture certainly wasn't mine to* break. Also, since you are now the most famous artist in history, your work has gotten really expensive, and one can't just go around knocking down expensive things every time one is mad.

Which brings me to the next part: why I did it. I have been thinking about this a lot, and it's hard to put it into words, so I thought I would use pictures. I chose five pictures for you because my school counselor (who you would probably want to sleep with) asked me for five, and I thought it was a good number. I hope all the pictures together will tell the story of what happened. It helped me understand. I don't expect you to forgive me, but I thought I owed you the truth, artist to artist, if I may.

When we get critiqued, our photo teacher makes us say no more than three words about our work, but we can't name anything that's in there. Here goes.

The first is about falling in love.

The second is about losing.

The third is about holding on.

The fourth is about the truth.

The fifth is about hope.

I welcome whatever you bring my way, be it a life-long curse or a flood of insults, and I am ready to face it with grace, humor, and quite a bit of strength. You see, Señor Picasso, I know this may sound dramatic, but I think I was dying there for a while, or at least disappearing, and your sculpture changed everything. I am the one who pushed it, yes, but you *are the one who made it. For that, you crazy bronze bender, I am forever grateful and at your service.*

*Yours, Miriam*

# Acknowledgments

*Grazie mamma and papa*, who filled our house with books and photographs and taught me to keep my heart and mind open, especially when it's hard.

My *fratello* and *sorelle*, who are my favorite characters in real life.

My *nonni*, whose spirits nudged me along.

My friends, who get it, and share, and look for me when I hide.

There's not enough room for the number of times I'd like to thank Kate McKean, for her guidance, patience, perseverance, and sense of humor. Thank you. Thank you.

Thank you, Brian, for taking Miriam on and helping me say what I mean, the ultimate goal (see Mr. Kite).

Thank you, Sandy, for aligning time, space, and language. Your work is priceless. And Mallory, for handing the book to the readers.

Thank you, Lanie and Dolores, who made it possible for me to sit and write.

A friend once told me a story about a girl who knocked over a Picasso on the National Mall. Thank you, Kerri, for giving me that seed. I've never met the girl, but thank you, wherever you are, for inspiring me with your moment.

My high school copy of Pablo Neruda's *Twenty Love Poems and a Song of Despair* (trans. W. S. Merwin) came back for Eva while writing this book. I'm grateful I could experience his words again.

I am indebted to the following people who read the early, terrible, long-buried versions of this book, especially

Meaghan, Erum, and Allison. I hope you like this one better. Also, Erika Mailman, who made me write an outline.

To Mr. Kite, who told me to *cut the crap* and *say what you mean*. Best advice ever.

To my students, whose courage and tenacity gave me zero excuses.

To my three beautiful children, who make and break my heart every day.

This book is dedicated to my husband, Benjamin, for all of it.

© Melissa Rauch Photography

## About the Author

Anna Pellicioli was born in Italy, the third of five children. Since then, she has moved to seven different countries, including France, Nepal, and Russia. She graduated from Barnard College and taught high school English and Literacy before starting to write books. She now lives in Istanbul with her husband and three children. Her other loves include walking in the woods, swimming in the ocean, and reading picture books aloud.